Cruel Summer

Also by Alyson Noël

# Cruel Summer

# Alyson Noël

St. Martin's Griffin ✥ New York

This is a work of fiction. All of the characters, organizations, and events portrayed in this novel are either products of the author's imagination or are used fictitiously.

www.stmartins.com

Book design by Spring Hoteling

ISBN-13: 978-0-312-35511-1
ISBN-10: 0-312-35511-4

10  9  8  7  6

*For Kate Schafer—agent extraordinaire and overall awesome person!*

## Acknowledgments

Big, huge, glittery, confetti-strewn thanks go to: Matthew Shear and Rose Hilliard, to whom I'm eternally grateful; Kate Schafer, for too many reasons to mention; Sandy Sherman, the perfect yang to my yin; and every single one of my readers—you guys totally rock!

Cruel Summer

*June 13*

*Dear Aunt Tally,*

*When I asked my mom for your e-mail address, she just laughed and told me you didn't have one. But I know she's just joking—right?*

*I mean, it's not like you have to have a computer or anything, since I'm planning on bringing my laptop anyway, I just need to make sure you have wi-fi, high speed, broadband, or whatever they call it where you live, since it's really important for me to stay connected,* ~~*because, well, I just started hanging with this new group of friends and*~~

*Anyway, so my mom just walked in and when she saw me writing to you she said, "Don't waste the postage, Colby. You'll get there long before that letter does." But just in case she's wrong, I'm sending it anyway. And just in case she's right, well, then I guess there's nothing more to say.*

*See you soon.*

*Love,*

*Colby*

*June 15*

*Dear Mom and Dad,*

*Just in case you decide to stop arguing long enough to come look for me, you should know that I'm <u>NOT</u> home. I'm out with my friends, determined to enjoy my <u>LAST NIGHT OF FREEDOM.</u>*

*Attempting one last stab at having a little <u>FUN</u> before you succeed in <u>TAKING IT ALL AWAY.</u>*

*But don't worry. I'm not running away or anything. Mostly because your decision to send me away makes running away seem almost redundant.*

*Besides, I've done my best to reason with you and try to put an immediate halt to all that you've started, but since I've so clearly failed, I will soon surrender, comply with your wishes, and resign myself to the fate you have so randomly chosen for me.*

*Only not now, later. Because now, I'm just going to try to enjoy myself—while I still can.*

*Though before I go I'd like to leave you with a few thoughts for you to consider:*

It's not too late!

There's plenty of time to reconsider!

Everything you've done can still be undone!

*At least take the time to think about it.*

*~Colby*

### COLBY'S JOURNAL FOR DESPERATE TIMES LIKE RIGHT NOW

June 16

I can't believe I'm actually writing in this journal. I mean, ~~today,~~ (well, technically it would now be yesterday), when my mom gave it to me, I just looked at her and said, "What's this?"

And she said, "I thought you could use it to write about all of the exciting things that happen to you this summer."

So then I shook my head, rolled my eyes, and sighed as loud as I could.

Then I tossed it onto my desk and watched it skid all the way across the top until it fell off the side and tumbled to the ground, as my mom just stood there, still and silent, gazing between the upside-down journal and me.

But I just narrowed my eyes and stared right back, wondering if she was going to yell at me, cry, or both.

But in the end she just shook her head and left my room. And the second the door closed behind her, I'm the one who started to cry.

Though not for too long, since I didn't want my face to be all puffy and red for the good-bye party Amanda was supposed to throw for me. Even though in the end it really wasn't much of a party since it pretty much consisted of a six-pack of her brother's beer, a bag of chips, and us.

Well, at least until she made a few calls—

Okay, I was just about to write the rest of the story, but then I decided to stop because it feels really weird to be confessing in this thing. I mean, as much as I'd like to write about <u>EVERYTHING</u> that just happened (and trust me, there's <u>PLENTY</u> to write about), because I'm thinking it might really help me to get it all down on paper and maybe even clear my head and put it all back in perspective, the thing is, I can't help but think—*what if someone reads it?*

I mean, it's not like you can password protect a leather-bound notebook.

Not to mention how I can <u>STILL</u> hear my parents totally yelling and screaming downstairs, which is not only making it hard to concentrate, but also freaking me out to think what will happen when they come up here to check on me while I sleep (because that's what they always do after they've exhausted themselves from one of their arguments and are ready to call it a night and head off to their separate rooms), and maybe even end up peeking at what I've written.

And even though I know that probably sounds totally paranoid, in light of how they've managed to wreck just about every aspect of my life, I think the breakdown in trust is completely justified.

So, with that in mind, it's better to just sign off for now and continue this at another time, in another place.

Or not.

June 16
Text Message:
To: Amanda
Message: This is the last txt msg Ull get from me bcuz IM packed N ready N lvg 4 LAX v soon so I wanna say bye N also 2 say last nite was soooo fun but it also makes lvg that much harder I still cant believe my rents

R doing this 2 me O well Plz say bye 2 Levi 4 me N plz
give him my email cuz I 4got 2
K, ttfn, Colby

*June 16*
*Dear Mom and Dad,*

*I really hope that by the time you return from dropping me off at the airport you will find this letter and realize what a big mistake you've made.*

*Because this is <u>NOT</u> fair!*

*It feels like <u>I'M</u> the one being punished because <u>YOU GUYS</u> decided to get a divorce—a divorce that, as you know, not only am I completely against, but that I definitely don't agree with. And yet, here I am, being banished from everything I know and love, and it just doesn't make any sense.*

*It's not like I'm the one causing trouble. It's not like I'm the one yelling and screaming and fighting all the time. Because that would be <u>YOU!</u> And yet, somehow, the plane ticket is still in my name.*

*I mean, did you ever stop to consider that maybe the <u>WRONG PERSON</u> is being sent to Aunt Tally's? Did you ever stop and think that maybe one of <u>YOU</u> should go cool off on a Greek island for a couple months, so I can just stay home and enjoy my summer in peace?*

*Apparently not.*

*I hope that by the time you finish this letter you will have come to your senses, stop fighting, see the error of your ways, and bring me back home immediately.*

*It's as simple as calling the airport and having me paged.*

*I will be listening for my name.*

*And even though it's probably not necessary to say, I want to assure you that should you choose to reverse your decision, I hereby do solemnly swear, to never mention this little digression again. I will just tuck it away in the file of Things We'd All Rather Forget.*

*But if not . . . then I'm afraid I can't be held responsible for my actions.*

*Please take the time to reconsider. And remember, it's never too late to correct a mistake.*

*Love,*

*Your sad, lonely, and already completely homesick daughter—*
*Colby*

## COLBY'S JOURNAL FOR DESPERATE TIMES WHEN SHE'S STUCK AT 37,000 FEET WHERE THERE IS NO INTERNET ACCESS

June 16

I tried. Really, I did. I gave it my best shot, but here I am anyway. Sitting on this stupid airplane, next to some stupid, smelly old man, in seat 37G, which is the second-to-last row, just around the corner from the toilets (which, believe me, I can totally smell) and right next to the window in case I want to open the shade and gaze out at—nothing. Seriously, there's nothing out there but miles and miles of white cloud tops.

That's how high up we are.

That's how far from home I am.

And it would all be fine and worth it if I was going to end up somewhere good, but I just happened to peek at the first page of the guidebook my dad slipped me at the airport and this is what it says:

*Tinos is the most important destination in Greece for religious pilgrims, and yet it remains one of the least commercialized islands.*

Um, excuse me? Religious pilgrims? Least commercialized? And those are the good things?

And if that wasn't bad enough, it then goes on to say:

*Tinos is also famous for its dovecotes—which are elaborate stone towers, with ornamental perches for doves.*

And then it waxes all rhapsodic over some stupid natural spring in some stupid main square in some stupid small village where the locals apparently:

*Wash their clothes by hand.*

So basically I guess you could say that my parents are sending me to a place where religious pilgrims, doves, and villagers all hand wash their delicates right smack in the middle of the town square.

And I don't think I need to point out how it really doesn't get any worse than that.

Not to mention how I did absolutely nothing to deserve any of this in the first place. Since it's not like I got in trouble, or did anything illegal or bad, and yet, here I am, the one being punished.

I mean, just because my parents decided to wreck their lives and get divorced shouldn't mean they get to wreck my life too. Isn't it enough that they're robbing me of a two-parent home, as well as their mutual guidance, stability, and security?

DO THEY REALLY HAVE TO WRECK MY ENTIRE FREAKING SUMMER TOO???

Apparently, they do.

Because according to my mom's shrink/life coach, I need to be "removed from all negative influences," and shielded from "any harmful issues that may arise during this turbulent time," so that my parents can "work out their issues in private," so I can return to a "peaceful household." Which may sound all fine and reasonable on paper, but here's the thing—how does she know what I'll return to? And how can she guarantee it'll be <u>PEACEFUL?</u>

And more importantly, <u>WILL I EVEN BE ABLE TO RECOGNIZE MY OWN LIFE ONCE I'M ALLOWED TO RETURN TO IT?</u>

Or will they have hacked away at it so much, that by the time I get back, there'll be nothing left that's even remotely familiar?

Because last night, when I came home from Amanda's, almost a full two hours past curfew, braced and ready for big-time trouble, my mom and dad were so involved in one of their never-ending arguments they didn't even notice I was back, much less late. Heck, they probably weren't even aware that I was even gone in the first place—that's how bad it's gotten.

And just as I was sneaking past the downstairs guest room (where my dad's been camping out for the last three months), and heading upstairs to my room, I completely froze, with my eyes bugged out and my jaw on the floor, as I distinctly heard them use the words—*sell the house—move*—and—*Cyber School.*

In. That. Order.

And now, because of that, pretty much all I can think about is:

1) If they fight like that when I'm gone just a few hours, how bad will it get when I'm gone for three months? Ten o'clock news bad? *Dateline* Special bad? I seriously wish I was joking, but I'm not.

2) Move? Who's moving? And more importantly—*where??*

3) What the heck is *Cyber School*? And how does it apply to *me*?

4) If they really care that much about my "peace of mind," then how can they banish me to no-man's land—just ship me off to live with an aunt, who, up until two weeks ago, they both referred to as "Crazy Aunt Tally?"

I'm totally serious. That's exactly what they called her, and they didn't even laugh when they said it. They'd say things like: "Your crazy aunt Tally sent you a birthday card," and then my dad would drop a blue airmail envelope onto my desk. Or, "Your crazy aunt Tally made you these earrings," then my mom would jiggle something dangly and beaded in her hand.

And now, just because they've decided they can no longer stand each other, can no longer communicate without screaming, crazy Aunt Tally is suddenly the perfect summer chaperone?

I mean, ARE THEY JOKING?

And just exactly HOW am I supposed to survive, for a WHOLE ENTIRE SUMMER, with no car, no cell phone, no Sidekick, no Sephora, no Abercrombie, no parties, no friends, and no Internet access???

Not to mention how this was supposed to be my best summer yet, the one I'd been working toward since practically forever. Because after years of going through the motions of a ho-hum existence, after years of being just another blank face in the crowd, I finally penetrated Amanda Harmon's inner circle. And I'm not talking clinging to the outer fringes along with all the other wannabe dorks; no I'm talking right inside the Promised Land. I'm talking the glorious, golden, inner sanctum of those who are allowed to hang at her house, ride in her car, and maintain a spot on her cell phone speed dial.

Though I'm still not sure how it happened. It's like, one moment, I'd been secretly worshipping her from afar, going all the way back to elementary school when I'd pretend to make fun of her hairstyles and mannerisms (but only because my one and only friend at the time truly did despise her, which made me feel like I had to hide the fact of how I wanted to be just like her), and the next, in a complete and total fluke which also turned out to be a moment of complete and total kismet, I'd scored the winning goal in a down and dirty game of fifth-period PE volleyball, after which she came right up to me and said, "Hey, way to score."

And then she high-fived me.

And then she complimented me on my brand-new Nikes.

And the next thing I knew, I was pretty much her new best friend.

Which kind of required me to get rid of my old best friend.

But since we were kind of in a fight anyways, I decided to go with it and never look back.

Anyway, all of this happened just in time for what was gearing up to be the most amazing summer of my, so far mostly unamazing seventeen years, which, now, because of my parents, their attorneys, and my mother's personal guidance counselor, has been tragically edited down to just one single night.

Still, as far as nights go, I have to admit it <u>WAS</u> pretty incredible (hence the two hours past curfew return!) and since it's most likely the only great night I'll ever get, I should probably write it all down so I'll always remember it.

Only not now, later. Because now, the flight attendants are bringing the meals and I'm starving.

*June 17*

*Dear Mom and Dad,*

*You may notice that this letter is written on a Coke-stained Ellas Ferry Lines cocktail napkin. Well, that's because I'm now on the boat to Tinos. That's right,* <u>*THE BOAT.*</u> *Because apparently there is no airport in Tinos, which means you are sending me to a place that planes refuse to land in.*

*Thanks for that.*

*Though what you may not have realized is that planes do land in Mykonos, lots of them. Which only makes me wonder why you couldn't have sent me there instead? Because according to the superhot Italian guy I sat next to on the flight from Athens to Mykonos (and his boyfriend),* <u>*NOBODY*</u> *goes to Tinos.*

*Nobody but, oh yah, that's right—*<u>*ME.*</u>

*At first I was thinking I'd use this napkin to get rid of my gum, but then I realized that would only deprive you of seeing the unhappy results of your decision.*

*Love,*

*The extremely unhappy but not like you care—*

*Colby*

COLBY'S JOURNAL FOR DESPERATE TIMES WHEN THE ELECTRICAL OUTLET IS SO WEIRD SHE CAN'T EVEN PLUG IN HER COMPUTER TO RECHARGE IT

June 18

I don't even know what time it is, much less what day. All I know is that I just woke up and it's dark out, but whether it's night dark or early morning dark, I can't be sure. The only thing I know is that my room looks like this:

Smooth white walls
White filmy curtains
White marble floors
White sheepskin rug on white marble floors
Single bed with white sheets and sky blue comforter
White bedside table with small silver lamp with sky
  blue shade

So basically, you could say it looks a lot like the view from seat 37G—nothing but white, white, white, with the occasional small pocket of blue. And oh yeah, the electrical outlet is all weird and different and absolutely refuses to cooperate with my computer plug, and it makes me wonder what the rest of the house is like too. I mean, I barely got a chance to see it, because the second my aunt Tally showed me my room, I pretty much fell face-first on my bed. Partly because I was tired from the twenty-two hours of nonstop traveling, and partly because crying always exhausts me like that.

That's right, I cried.

In public.

Like the world's most pathetic baby.

It's like, the second I'd finished writing that napkin letter to my parents I felt so angry and frustrated and sad, I just broke down in tears. And even though I knew it was stupid and embarrassing and childish, I couldn't stop. I guess it just needed to come out, so there wasn't much I could do about it.

But when I finally calmed down enough to look around, I noticed this really old lady dressed in all black, and she was totally staring at me, though not in a kind grand-motherly way like you'd think. So I grabbed my bags and went outside, where I stood on deck, gazing back at where I came from, wondering what would happen if I just turned around and took the next boat back to Mykonos, found a job, a place to live, and settled in without ever contacting anyone to tell them where I am and what I'm up to. Just start over, build a new life, and grow old. Never to return.

I mean, how would my parents feel <u>THEN?</u>

It's funny how just fantasizing about getting revenge can actually make you feel better. So after imagining my parents so frantic with grief, worry, and guilt they vow to halt the divorce and bring me back home, I wiped my face and gazed toward Tinos, and that's when I noticed this really cute guy standing just a few feet away.

And just as I thought—*hey, maybe things are starting to look up, maybe this won't be so bad after all,* I glanced down at my hands and saw how they were all black, and inky, and streaked with mascara, which meant that my face was prob-ably all black, and inky, and streaked with mascara too. Which was probably the only reason he was even looking at me to begin with. So I ran back inside to search for a bath-room so I could clean myself up, but then right when I found one, the horn blew, and from the way everyone stampeded for the exit, I figured it meant we were there.

It's weird how I recognized my aunt right away even though the last time I saw her I was just two, and it's not like I can even remember that time. But still, I just took one look at her and I *knew*. Though it's not because she looked like someone's crazy aunt. It was more because she looks a lot like my mom. Well, if my mom was relaxed and happy, and had kept her original nose, and let her blond bob grow back out to its natural brown waviness, and then dressed in beachwear all the time and not just when she was actually at the beach or by the pool.

Okay, so I just looked outside again and I'm guessing it's A.M. since the sun is now rising. So I think I'll stop writing and go outside, and try to figure out just where the heck I am.

## Twenty Minutes Later:

Okay, all I know is this—I can totally see part of Mykonos from here. And let me just say that even at a distance I can tell it's a helluva lot better than this place.

I'm so screwed.

I think Tally just woke up.

## Twelve Hours Later:

How I Spent My First Day in ~~Prison~~ Greece

1) I woke up (duh).
2) I wrote in my journal.

3) I went exploring on my own and discovered that I am surrounded by: dirt, white houses, geraniums, more dirt, rocks, and if I crane my neck a certain way I have a pretty good view of both the sea and Mykonos—which, I can tell just from looking, is a gazillion times better than here.

4) I got through a very awkward breakfast with my aunt Tally that consisted of bread with butter and honey, along with a completely horrible cup of coffee that not only tasted like mud but actually <u>TURNED INTO MUD</u> when I let it sit too long. Seriously! And I did everything in my power not to vomit that first sip back up (because that would be both rude and gross). Though I think Tally could tell by my face how much I hated it, because she just started laughing and said I was under no obligation to finish it. And all I can say is if the rest of Greece is as bad as their coffee, then this summer is going to suck even more than I thought.

5) During breakfast Tally tried to get me to open up about the divorce, but luckily, when I made it clear it wasn't on my list of favorite things to talk about, she let it go. Then she just started talking about herself, and how she came here fourteen years ago and never looked back. And when I asked her why she didn't go to Mykonos instead, she just shook her head and said

that wasn't her scene. Which I took to mean that she has a very high tolerance for boredom, because from what I've seen so far, that's about all this place has to offer.

6) After breakfast, I tried to be polite and help with the dishes, but Tally just shook her head and waved me away so I went back to my room where I took a shower and unpacked.

7) After, we walked into town (um, if you can even call it a "town," I mean, it's really more like a tiny village, but whatever) so Tally could show me where her shop (where she sells her jewelry and stuff), the bank, the market, and a couple other places I might need are located—even though they're pretty much all lined up on the same small street. And when I asked her where the big stores are, you know like the department stores and stuff, she just laughed and said, "In Athens."

8) After my tour of the town, we walked back home and got in her jeep and then she drove me all around the island so I could look at more dirt, more geraniums, more rocks, and more white houses.

9) And after two hours of that, she asked me if I wanted to go to the beach, but I just shook my head and told her I was jet-lagged. And even though I'm not really sure what being jet-lagged actually feels like, I'm thinking if it resembles

anything remotely like sadness, depression, and complete and overwhelming despondency, then I totally was not lying.

10) In the evening, I emerged from my ~~prison cell~~ room just long enough to have a dinner of Greek salad (~~decent,~~ no, good actually, though by no means great) and some Greek casserole dish that I won't even try to pronounce, much less spell, but that tasted like some seriously messed-up lasagna. And then I said good night, and went back to bed.

The End.

P.S. The good news is I have about seventy-five more days ahead of me that promise to be exactly like this one. Yippee!

COLBY'S JOURNAL FOR DESPERATE TIMES WHEN THERE'S NO LOGICAL EXPLANATION FOR WHAT IS HAPPENING TO HER

June 19

Okay, so apparently my mom was *not* joking. And I didn't mention this before because I was really hoping that she and Tally were in cahoots, playing some kind of messed-up mind game. But evidently, I'm completely cut off from the outside world. Because not only does my aunt Tally not have a computer or Internet access, but she also does not have a TV. Which is so completely weird, not to mention practically impossible to get used to. I mean, even though the shows are probably all in Greek, which I wouldn't be able to understand anyway, not having access to a television just doesn't seem right.

Though it does explain why my parents refer to her as *Crazy*.

But unfortunately, that's not even the half of it, because believe me, there's more. For example:

1) She talks to her plants. Seriously, she thanks them for blossoming, growing, and basically doing all of the things they're supposed to be doing anyway. And when she caught me gaping at her with my jaw hanging down to my knees, watching in complete and total disbelief as she whispered sweet nothings to her geraniums, she just turned and explained (with a totally straight face) that they're *alive and aware*. And even though I'm clearly not doubting the *alive* part, since all the leaves are green and not brown, it's the *aware* part that worries me. I mean, aware of *what* exactly? So when I asked her which language they respond in—Greek or English, she just smiled in that weird peaceful way and kept at it.

2) She only keeps what she can use. Which sounds completely reasonable until she goes on to explain that collecting and acquiring things you don't *truly* need only results in "clogged energy."

Which also means that the moment she finishes a book (and she reads like, one a day) she thanks it for the knowledge it provided (believe me, I wish I was joking but I'm not) and then she passes it on to someone else. Same with CDs, clothes, you name it, nothing gets saved, it all gets thanked, blessed, and passed on to the next recipient. Which basically means this house is so spare and empty it feels like we're living in a monastery—only without the vow of silence, since we do get to talk (especially to plants and other inanimate objects). Though the truth is, I really wouldn't mind a vow of silence since I don't have much to say anyway. Mostly because I'm too busy worrying about how I'll possibly survive the next seventy-four days (and counting!), to focus on something as trivial as small talk.

3) She's totally in cahoots with my mom's shrink and thinks it's just wonderful that I'm escaping my parents' "negative energy" as well as taking a break from my "computer addiction and obsessive focus on accumulation and mass consumerism." Whatever the heck that means.

I mean, she's nice and all, don't get me wrong, and she means well, I can tell. But the freaky thing is that she actually *believes* all of this stuff. And while that may be all fine and good for her, the fact remains that she's the one who <u>CHOSE</u> to live this austere, serene island life, while I myself did <u>NOT</u>. And even though I just got here, I don't think it's too big of a stretch to say that it's really not working for me.

Because what my aunt obviously does not understand is how imperative it is for me to stay in touch with Amanda. How it's seriously and completely crucial that Amanda does <u>NOT</u> forget me while I'm gone. There's just too much riding on our friendship, too much at stake. I mean, if I'm going to have any fun at all during my last year of high school, if I want to go to prom, and parties, and basically partake in anything worth partaking in, then <u>I HAVE TO STAY TIGHT WITH AMANDA!</u>

I <u>CANNOT</u> allow her to replace me with some undeserving wannabe. I just can't afford to let that happen.

And the reason I'm so worried about it in the first place, is because I happen to know for a fact that Amanda has the attention span of a housefly. Seriously, she's always flitting from one object to another, unable to stay focused on any one thing. Like she has social ADD or something. And now that I'm gone I'm afraid she'll just land on someone else, and come September, all of my hard work will be wasted.

Like on Friday, my last night in town, when we were sitting in her room, flipping through magazines and listening to music (which is pretty much all she could be bothered to arrange for my big going-away party), and right after I read our horoscopes out loud, she looked at me and squinted and went, "Wait—so where are you going again?"

And honestly, I could hardly believe it. I mean, it's not like I hadn't told her like a million times already, but it's not like I could actually say that either. So I just mentally rolled my eyes, tucked my long, brown hair behind my ears, and then gazed at her perfect face, which was perfectly framed by the perfect smoke ring she just blew, and said, "Greece." Then I watched as she shrugged, grabbed a chunk of her bleached blond hair, and bent it toward her nose, brushing the ends against its dainty, slightly upturned tip.

"I don't get it. Why Greece? Why not somewhere good? You know, like Cabo or Cancun or something?" she said, dropping her hair and switching her attention to her French-manicured nails.

But I just shrugged. I mean, it really wasn't worth explaining how I only had one crazy aunt, and she just happened to live on a Greek island nobody's ever heard of. But when I saw Amanda staring at me like that, you know, with her lips all pursed and her eyebrows raised, I knew I had to at least try to explain. "It's an island, and it's supposed to be really pretty," I said, amazed to hear myself actually defending it. But then that's how I always feel around Amanda, like I need to prove my right to exist.

But she just reached for her phone and flipped it open. And just as I thought she was looking for a way to evict me, she scrolled through her contacts and said, "Levi's going to Greece. Let's call him."

<u>LEVI BONHAM!</u> The uber-hot guy I've been lusting after since he moved to our town back when I was just a nerdy little sixth-grader and he was already a smoking hot twelve-year-old, who also happens to be the other major reason for why I desperately need to stay connected.

Seriously, Levi is the most gorgeous guy I've ever seen (okay, maybe not including magazines, TV, and/or movies), but still, he's so amazingly hot it's surreal. He's like the male equivalent of Amanda. And luckily for me, Amanda doesn't like him like THAT, because if she did I wouldn't have stood a chance. But for whatever reason she lusts after his less hot but still cute friend, Casey Sayers. And all she had to do was place the call, and five minutes later, just like magic, they appeared.

And it's not like I haven't hung out with Levi before, because ever since I started hanging with Amanda I've had access to a whole host of things I used to only dream about. But still, it's not like we ever really exchanged more than a few words, or in his case—mumbles.

That's right, as perfect as I think Levi Bonham is, even I have to admit, he has one minor flaw—he's not much of a talker, he's way more of a mumbler. But then again, when you're that gorgeous, conversational skills aren't really required.

But since I'm not at all gorgeous, since I'm pretty much an average girl (okay, maybe I'm just *slightly* better than average since I'm more or less thin, and my skin is more or less clear, and my hair is pretty much just brown and normal, and nothing on my face really stands out in either a super positive or super negative way—which makes me pretty much the opposite of the blond, tan, and blue-eyed Amanda), I'm kind of forced to keep my small-talk abilities honed and sharpened.

I mean, in my case, showing up and standing around just isn't enough. Which means the last few times we hung out, I was forced to work overtime just trying to get him to laugh, which was completely impossible until I inadvertently tripped and fell smack onto the coffee table, which resulted in him doubling over in laughter and gasping for air, for a full five minutes. But for the rest of the time after that, I mostly just tried to ask a lot of questions about his favorite sports, favorite cars, and all kinds of other stuff that he's obviously into, but that I really don't care about.

But even so, the most I ever got for my attempts were a couple of mumbles and a grunt or two.

Until last Friday night when:

<u>I HOOKED UP WITH LEVI BONHAM!!!!!</u>

It's like, one minute we were sitting awkwardly on the couch, side by side, pretending to watch TV while Amanda and Casey were doing who knows what upstairs in her room, and the next thing I know <u>LEVI BONHAM WAS PRETTY MUCH ON TOP OF ME!</u>

Though it's not like he just pounced or anything crude like that. It was way more romantic and actually kind of cute the way he acted like he was reaching for his glass, but then somehow ended up smack on my lips.

And even though it was a little awkward at first, I mean trying to figure out where our lips and tongues should go, it wasn't long before I was totally into the zone of how he kisses, and the next thing I knew, I'd glanced at my watch and it was two hours past my curfew!

Only that's not entirely true.

Because the truth is, I was kind of worried about my curfew pretty much the entire time. I mean, even though kissing Levi was a completely amazing, dream-come-true kind of moment, the fact is, I couldn't stop worrying about my parents—wondering if they were still fighting, wondering if they'd managed to kill each other yet (joking, but not entirely).

But now, looking back, I wish I hadn't even bothered. I mean, it's not like they even noticed I was gone, and here I'd wasted a good part of my Levi Bonham Experience worrying about two people who obviously don't care all that much about me.

But after he tried to take off my dress for like the tenth time in a row, I pointed at my watch and told him I had to leave. And when I saw the way he just rolled his amazing blue eyes as he rolled right off of me, I thought:

*What the heck are you doing, Colby? I mean, hello, now's your big chance, the moment you've been waiting for! So what if you don't love him? Love never lasts anyway—just look at your parents! Not to mention how you're totally gonna regret it if you let him slip away!*

So then I reached for his hand and said, "Okay, maybe just a few more minutes."

And in the end, that's pretty much all it took.

Because the second it was over, he was already opening another beer before I'd even had a chance to adjust my dress, and when I finally stood and grabbed my purse and my keys, part of me couldn't help but wonder if it really did happen.

I guess I always thought The Big Moment would be, well, bigger.

And better.

And way more special than it actually was.

And I guess that's why I've put off writing about it until now. I mean, at the beginning of the night, when we first started kissing, I would occasionally open my left eye to peek at him, just so I could confirm that, yes, hard as it was to believe, I, Colby Catherine Cavendish, was totally locking lips, swapping spit, and playing big-time tonsil hockey with the hottest guy in school. And when I saw the way his eyes were closed so tight, and felt the way his lips were pressed so hard against mine, well, I couldn't help but feel like the luckiest girl in the world.

Despite the nagging voice in my head going—*why* YOU *Colby?*

*You're not hideous but you're not exactly hot. You test smart but it's not like he cares. Just because you're friends with Amanda doesn't mean you're cool. So out of all the girls he knows, out of all the superhot girls he could be making out with at this exact moment,* WHY YOU?

And honestly, I just didn't have an answer.

I still don't. Though I am firmly committed to no longer thinking about it.

Because even if it's just that he was bored on a Friday night and looking for something to do, it still doesn't explain why just seconds before I left he reached into the bowl of Doritos, grabbed a handful, looked me right in the eye, and said, "Hey, maybe I'll catch you in Greece. I might be going on a cruise or something."

Though it does explain why I plan to spend my entire

summer in the Internet café, waiting for some kind of contact or news of his arrival.

Waiting for proof that I didn't waste my virginity on someone who's bound to forget me.

*June 20*
*Dear Aunt Tally,*

*If you come home for ~~lunch~~ siesta and I'm not here it's because I'm at the Internet café. (Yup, I found it! Even though I know you were hoping I wouldn't!) Which means I probably won't be back in time to go to the beach with you today, and I hope you're not too upset about that.*

*Anyway, I just didn't want you to worry about me, because I think you'll find that I'm pretty self-sufficient, very independent, and really don't require all that much guidance. Which means you can just go about your business and act like I'm not even here, because I probably won't be around the house all that much anyway now that I know about the café.*

*Okay, well, have a good day—*
*Love,*
*Colby*

*June 20*
*Dear Mom and Dad,*

*Sorry I haven't written until now, I guess time flies when you're not having any fun.*

*Don't be fooled by the picture on the front of this postcard, because the truth is it's really not that pretty here and I've yet to see this beach.*

*Just in case you are questioning your decision, or have any lingering regrets about sending me here, then I'd like to inform you that I'm willing to return at any time with no hard feelings, and no questions asked.*

*Seriously, scout's honor.*

*But if you insist on standing by your choice, if you suffer no guilt, no remorse, no qualms, no regrets, no worries, and no self-doubt, then all I have to say is this:*

*I, Colby Catherine Cavendish, do hereby solemnly swear to give you (my parents) joint custody of this postcard so that you can spend alternating weekends and holidays with it, sparing you the burden of meeting in a predetermined, neutral location, with your respective lawyers in tow, who would gleefully charge you thousands of dollars just to tear it in half and hand each of you an equal-sized piece.*

*Love,*

*Your former daughter, now orphaned—*

*Colby*

June 20
To: AmandaStar
From: ColbyCat
Re: Ya'Sou!
Hey Amanda—

In case UR Idering Ya'Sou means both hi & bye here in Greece, kinda like Aloha in Hawaii. At least I think that's what it means!

NEway, jus wanted 2 say hey since I'm soooo far from U & I don't want U guyz 2 4get me! ☺

I'm still thinking about Fri bcuz it was sooooo fun & I totally cud've stayed even L8r since no1 even noticed I was L8. O well.

Tell Levi hi from me & tell him 2 msg me & tell me if he's still maybe coming 2 Greece like he sez.

But don't tell him about the totally hot guy I sat next 2 on the plane 2 Greece! ☺

L8R

Colby

P.S. Oh yah—almost 4got 2 tell U I'm starting a blog so u guyz can c my pics & stuff! So stop by & ck it out & don't 4get 2 tell Levi!

## CRUEL SUMMER

**Blogger Profile:**

Name—Colby Catherine (Cat)
Age—17
Gender—Just a girl
Sign—Peace
Industry—Adolescence
Occupation—Prisoner of Greece
Location—Tinos via sunny CA

**About me:**

I'm a seventeen-yr-old girl who's being punished by her parents. Banished from everything she knows and loves and packed off to spend the summer on a Greek island—which, trust me, is far worse than you could ever imagine.

The purpose of this blog is so that I can document the most horrible summer of my whole entire life, and share a few photos (think of it as evidence!) along the way.

Interests—Going home immediately!

Favorite Movie—Best movie ever, hands down, I don't care if it's old—*Breakfast at Tiffany's*. Even though the ending in the book version is actually way more realistic than the movie version, because it's not all sappy and sweet, and is more like real life and not how Hollywood likes to portray real life. But still, either way, Holly Golightly kicks ass!

Favorite Song—Um, this changes all the time, though my all-time favorite would probably be that song "Breathe" (don't judge me!) because it pretty much sums up my view of life, which is: bad things happen, people betray you, mistakes are made, parents divorce, and in the end there's nothing you can do to erase it, you can't rewind, can't go back, the only thing you can do is breathe. (And if you can't even do that then it really doesn't matter anyway, does it?) And no, I'm not being negative, just realistic.

Favorite Book—Other than *Breakfast at Tiffany's*, I have to say that I love to read just about anything and everything except for those BORING, wordy, never-ending novels written by old dead Russians that English teachers just love to assign and make you write papers on! But other than that, it's (mostly) all good!

## CRUEL SUMMER

June 20

Um, testing, 1, 2, 3, testing . . . Okay, so this is the official kickoff to my summer blogging project where I will share all of the occasionally awesome, but probably mostly horrific and boring things I'm doing and experiencing here on the Greek island of Tinos, which is famous for its religious pilgrims and superdeluxe dove condos but not much else.

But since, so far, I really haven't done much of anything (I mean, unpacking, sleeping, and searching for a place to log on isn't really worth writing about), I've decided to share a few pictures instead, so you can get an idea of what I'm dealing with here.

Ready? Here goes:

1) That's the outside of my aunt Tally's house where I'm staying. And believe it or not, they all pretty much look exactly like that. Seriously, they're all boxy, with white walls and colored doors and shutters, and they're all really stark and simple and no-nonsense. Which is pretty much the exact opposite of what I'm used to seeing back home.

2) That's my room—again, notice all the white. They're really big on white here. Though luckily that bed is more comfortable than it looks. I mean, it's way more narrow than my bed at home, but at least the pillow is halfway decent. Also, notice the evil-eye

pendant hanging over my bed? That's so I don't get "eye sick." You know, cursed by a jealous, hateful person with bad intent (which believe it or not, is something the locals take as a serious threat to one's overall well-being). And all I can say to that is: <u>IF YOU'RE CRAZY ENOUGH TO BE JEALOUS OF ME, THEN YOU ARE MORE THAN WELCOME TO WEAR MY SHOES AND TRADE PLACES SO I CAN GO HOME AND GET BACK TO MY REGULARLY SCHEDULED LIFE!</u>

3) If you think you're just looking at a photo of an old lady dressed all in black, and riding a donkey, then look again. Notice the basket hanging off the side of the donkey's butt? Guess what? It's filled with eggs. That's right, ladies and gentlemen, this is how you buy your eggs in Tinos. Via donkey. Delivered fresh, right to your door.

4) See that orangey-looking, round, runny lump? That's an egg yolk. Have you ever seen such a color? I know I haven't.

5) That's a picture of the Internet café where I'll be spending most all of my free time, sending e-mails, surfing the Net, and writing this blog. Notice the white walls and green shutters, then go back and reread #1 so you'll know that everything you read in this blog is legitimate and true and I'm not making anything up.

6) That's the table where I always sit and drink my Nescafé frappe—which is kind of like a foamy,

prehistoric Starbucks-type drink, only not near as good, though I am getting used to it. Mostly because I have no choice. Just like I'm trying to get used to everything around here because trust me, everything is really weird and different and, well, <u>FOREIGN</u>. And even though I know that's pretty much the whole point of traveling to another country, please keep in mind that I didn't exactly beg to come here. I was perfectly fine and happy at home, and I really wasn't looking for any new experiences.

7) This is the chair I sit on while I surf the Net, send e-mails, write letters and postcards, and blog. Notice how it's made of wood, which, by the way, makes it <u>VERY</u> uncomfortable after more than two hours of sitting. And I should know, since I've already done some major butt-in-chair time (see above about how I spend most all my free time). To the point where I'm actually thinking about bringing my own cushion in, since Petros refuses to provide one for me.

8) That's a picture of Petros, he's the owner of this café. You'd think he'd be glad to have some regular business for a change, but every morning when I come in, he takes one look at me, shakes his head, and says, "You are too white. You must to go outside and get some color. This is not good, not healthy." And then I tell him how that's really no way to treat your best customer, and to please

bring me a frappe because I have an Internet life to get back to. Then we both laugh, and he brings me my drink, but it's pretty obvious that he really wasn't joking and he seriously does not approve.

9) That's a picture of my aunt Tally's shop. It's right here in town, just a few doors down, at the end of the street. She makes jewelry and T-shirts and sells them to tourists. She also has some of her boy-friend's (Tassos's) pottery and sculptures in there as well, but only a few pieces since the shop is kind of small as you can see. Only I haven't met him yet because he's out of town. And I don't hang in her shop all that much anyway because it's usually pretty busy and I just end up feeling like I'm in the way.

10) That's my aunt Tally sitting on her terrace watch-ing the sunset and having a glass of wine. Most of the sunsets here are really stunning like that—like a blaze of purple, orange, and red, streaking the sky before dropping into the sea. But you get used to it pretty quick.

11) That's a picture of the Meltemi wind. Yes, the wind is so strong here that not only does it have a name, but you can actually photograph it. Just look at those swaying shrubs and giant swirls of dirt. Well, just so you know, it blows like this practically every day! Aunt Tally refers to it as "nature's air-conditioning" and says I'll be sweating big-time when it stops. All I know is that I want it to stop.

12) Oops, there is no #12. Aren't you glad? Because this blog is truly <u>PATHETIC,</u> believe me, I know.

But please stay tuned, because you never know, it just might get better (though I seriously doubt it!):
Comment me! (Please!)
Colby

*June 21*
*Dear Tally,*
*Sorry, but no beach for me today, I'm off to the café.*
*Hope you have a good day—*
*Love,*
*Colby*

June 21
To: AmandaStar
From: ColbyCat
Re: Hey!
OMG, those pics U sent frm ur party R HILARIOUS! They made me soooo homesick! And no, Petros from the café is so NOT my boyfriend, bcuz plz, he's like 40, & trst me there's way hotter guyz here! And also no, most of the guys here don't have mustaches like that, it's mostly just the old ones.
Spkg of—Jus Idering if UV heard NEthing from Levi? Did U give him my e-mail? And do U no if he's still maybe coming here on that cruise? If U talk to him tell him 2 msg me, k? Bcuz IM going completely crazy here with no car, no phone, no

good shops, no fast food, etc. etc. etc. and I really need 2 b in touch w/all my friends cuz I feel like I'm so far away it's like I'm on another planet!

Also, who was that girl with him in that one pic? U no by the pool? Do we know her? Bcuz it looked like she wuz all over him. ☹

Okay, got 2 go—miss u!

Colby

COLBY'S JOURNAL FOR DESPERATE TIMES LIKE WHEN THE ELECTRICITY GOES OUT FOR SO LONG THE INTERNET CAFÉ CLOSES FOR AN EVEN EARLIER SIESTA THAN USUAL

June 21

Um, excuse me, but am I the only one around here who's concerned by the way the hot water just inexplicably runs out in the middle of my shower, how the electricity works only when it wants (which is hardly ever), and how just about everything in this crazy place shuts down between the hours of two and five?

Because earlier today, I was in the café, blogging my heart out and minding my own business, when all of a sudden_____.

That's right, lights out, computer dead (as was my battery), I mean, a total flatline, code-blue moment. And not only did I lose my blog in progress (which was brilliant by the way, I mean, seriously the best thing I've ever written, not that anyone will ever see it now), but when I looked at Petros and raised both hands in the air, mimicking the international sign for—*What the heck?* all he did was shrug and say, "No problem, no problem, relax, it comes back."

And after what seemed like an hour of "relaxing," it still wasn't back. But he didn't seem too upset. Actually, he almost seemed happy, because he just kicked me out—seriously, he just walked right up to me, grabbed me by the sleeve, and dragged me to the door (with a big smile on his face the whole entire time I might add!). Then he flipped the sign over from OPEN to CLOSED (well, it's in Greek, but I assume that's what it says), pushed me outside, locked the door, and I just stood in the middle of the road, in a complete state of shock, watching as he practically skipped down the street, happy to be on his way to doing whatever the heck he does between the hours of two and five.

And since I haven't really been here all that long, I really didn't know what to do with myself. I mean, usually I pretty much just spend my days going back and forth from my room at my aunt's to the café. But this time, for whatever reason, I felt like taking a walk. So I wandered along the harbor and was thinking about stopping for yet another frappe at one of those cute little outdoor cafés, but since I didn't really feel comfortable with the idea of sitting all by myself like a big, lonely, friendless loser (even though I am), I decided to stop by my aunt Tally's shop where she sells all the jewelry and stuff she makes for tourists. But even though she seemed happy enough to see me, it was obvious she was really busy, so I just waved good-bye and headed back home, staring across the harbor, gazing at

Mykonos, knowing just by looking that they had no short-age of electricity over there, while wondering, yet again, why, <u>WHY</u> did I have to get stuck in this awful, primitive place?

And just as I was walking along the narrow dirt road that leads to the house, these two guys rode by on this old beat-up Vespa, coming so close they practically sideswiped me. Seriously, I could actually feel one of their sleeves brush right against mine as they passed. And just as I was about to yell something, the guy who was riding on the back turned and smiled.

And I stopped in my tracks and stared, knowing I recognized him from somewhere. But from where I couldn't imagine, because it's not like I really go anywhere outside of my aunt's house and the café, which also means I don't really know anyone other than Tally and Petros.

But it wasn't until I was back in my room, lying on my bed and gazing out the window that I realized it was the cute guy I saw on the boat.

*June 22*
*Dear Mom,*

*I know Dad moved out but since I don't have his address yet (probably because he still hasn't sent it) I'm hoping that you or your lawyer (yes, I got your letter about how you and Dad are only speaking via legal counsel) can pass this on when you're finished.*

*And just in case you're at all curious, I <u>have</u> been to the beach on the front of this postcard, and that's pretty much what it looks* like—no shops, no bars, no restaurants, no boardwalk—nothing but sand and water. Though I guess it's still kind of pretty—if you like barren landscapes, like that.

Please don't forget to pass this on to Dad, okay?

Love,

Your daughter who is doing her best to adjust to the lot you have given her,

Colby

June 22
To: AmandaStar
From: ColbyCat
Re: Hi!
Hey Amanda,

So, that Penelope chick? The one in the pic who was hanging all over Levi? Does she go 2 another school? Bcuz I don't know her and I'm jus Idering & U never really said.

Well, all my news is pretty much in my blog, so U should totally stop by and comment me!

Write back!

Ciao—

Colby

P.S. NE news from Levi???

## CRUEL SUMMER

June 24

So this is a picture of me (duh!) with my aunt Tally and her boyfriend, Tassos, whom I only just met because

he was out of town for the last week "on business."
Though to be honest, I think he was just trying to give
me and Tally some time and space to get to know each
other before he came on the scene.

It's funny how they kind of look like brother and
sister, huh? I mean, they're both tan, both have dark,
wavy hair, both have brown eyes, and, um, strong
noses (not a judgment, just a fact). But I know there's
no relation since no one in my family tree is Greek, but
Tassos is. He's actually from here, which makes him a
Tinian. Anyway, they've been together for like, twelve
years or something, though they're not married and it
doesn't seem like either one of them even really notices
that they're not married. I mean, they act like they're
married (except they don't fight), so when I asked them
why they don't just go ahead and do it already, they
both just shrugged and at the exact same moment,
said, "It's not necessary." And then I thought about my
own mom and dad, who even though they're busy getting unmarried, still can't seem to stop yelling and
screaming at each other, and I just shrugged too.

I mean, maybe they're right, since everything's so
temporary anyway, since everything has a beginning,
middle, and end. So it's probably better just to leave the
door open, since you never know when you'll need to
use it.

Anyway, I've already forgotten the name of this
beach, but I guess it doesn't really matter since it's not
like you'd know it, and I probably wouldn't be able to

spell it anyway—in either alphabet. I mean, even though everyone says Greek is phonetic, the second I see all those bizarre-looking letters, I'm lost. But all you really need to know about this beach is that it's absolutely <u>NOTHING</u> like our beaches at home. Seriously.

For starters, all of the beaches here are just beaches. They don't double as food courts or minimalls or gyms like most of ours do.

And second, there are living, breathing, ocean-dwelling creatures that can be found pretty close to shore, which is also unlike our beaches.

So, like the moment we got our towels all laid out and I started to settle in, Tassos tossed me some fins, a mask, a snorkel, and a large net bag, and told me to follow behind and stay close, but not too close.

And as we headed out into the water (which, I might add, is much easier here since there are no waves to dive under; seriously, the water is completely flat), I put on my gear and did my best to keep up while he swam way out by the rocks, searching for octopus and sea urchin, which, to be honest, I really doubted we'd find because it just seemed too weird to think there were octopus lurking around out there since I guess I always think of them as living <u>WAY, WAY OUT THERE,</u> like more in a place you can only reach by boat or submarine, and less in a place you can access with a snorkel and a pair of fins. But believe it or not, there was plenty to choose from and I watched in amazement as he proceeded to catch three of them, with nothing more than HIS BARE HANDS (!), before tossing them into the bag I was carrying.

I'd also like to mention that the whole entire time Tassos and I were swimming, my aunt Tally was lying on the beach, reading one of her many books, COMPLETELY TOPLESS!

Seriously!

And believe me, I wish I was kidding, but from what I've seen around here so far, pretty much everyone goes topless at the beach.

Well, everyone BUT ME!

And I can't imagine I ever will. I mean, it's just too weird, and it made me really uncomfortable. I seriously couldn't even look at my aunt until it was time to leave and she put her T-shirt back on.

So then later, after we got back home and we all took showers and stuff, Tassos prepared the octopus and put together a big Greek salad, while I helped Tally peel a bunch of potatoes so we could make homemade french fries. And then they poured some wine (yup, they even let me have a glass!) and put on a Beatles CD (oh yeah, I forgot to mention that she has no problem with music, just television) and we ate our meal outside and sang that old song, "Here Comes the Sun."

Only we changed the words to "There Goes the Sun" because while we were eating we were watching it set.

And even though it probably sounds pretty dorky

and lame (I mean, it was totally and completely dorky), in some weird way, it was also kind of fun.

But that's only because it's so boring around here, that's pretty much the best you can hope for.

The only bad thing is I didn't get to the Internet café until now. And since it's pretty late, Petros has spent the last five minutes giving me the international sign to skedaddle—which basically means he is now standing by the door and waving at me to get out. Which also means he's just thirty seconds away from marching right over and grabbing my sleeve.

I swear, the customer service totally sucks around here!

Anyway, before I go I should mention that the last picture is of me eating octopus—which I know is probably pretty self-explanatory, but still, it is kind of hard to believe. I mean, I never thought I'd see the day, because—gag!

And trust me, the only reason I'm smiling is because Tassos was holding the camera and I didn't want to make him feel bad.

Besides, you know what they say—"When in Greece . . ."

Okay, Petros is now yanking on my sleeve, muttering something in Greek. And even though I have no idea what he's saying, trust me, the subtext is not good.

So . . . Good night!

Please, please, comment me!

Colby

*June 25*
*Dear Dad,*

   *Thanks for finally sending me your new address, though I
have to say it seems really weird to imagine you living in an apartment. I mean, can you hear the neighbors upstairs? And how big
is it? Is there a separate room for me, for when I come visit?*

   *Also, I've been thinking—now that you are officially out of the
house and no longer arguing with Mom except through your lawyers, I thought maybe it would be okay if I come home. And it's not
just because I'm feeling homesick (though I won't lie to you, Dad, I
am), but I think Mom might really need me to help her through this
difficult time. I mean, since you refuse to talk to each other you probably aren't aware of this, but from her last letter I could really sense
her loneliness, and I think she might really need me.*

   *Though I want to make it clear that I'm telling you this in the
strictest confidence, because I'm sure she wouldn't want you to know.
So let's just keep this between us and please don't make any mention of it to either her or your attorney.*

   *If you'd like, you can either overnight the ticket, or arrange for
me to pick it up at the ticket counter.*

   *Either way, I'm sure Aunt Tally will understand.*

   *See you soon—*

   *Love,*

   *Colby*


*June 25*
*Dear Mom,*

   *Just wanted to wish you a good time on your yoga retreat!*

   *Also, I've been thinking—now that Dad is officially out of* the house and you two are no longer arguing except through your lawyers, I thought maybe it would be okay if I come home. And it's not just because I'm feeling homesick (though I won't lie to you, Mom, I am), but I think Dad might really need me to help him through this difficult time. I mean, since you refuse to talk to each other you probably aren't aware of this, but from his last letter I could really sense his loneliness, and I think he might really need me.

Though I want to make it clear that I'm telling you this in the strictest confidence, because I'm sure he wouldn't want you to know. So let's just keep this between us and please don't make any mention of it to either him or your attorney.

If you'd like, you can either overnight the ticket, or arrange for me to pick it up at the ticket counter.

Either way, I'm sure Aunt Tally will understand.

See you soon—

Love,

Colby

June 26
To: AmandaStar
From: ColbyCat
Re: Um, remember me?
Hey Amanda,

Jus ckg in 2 say hey B cuz I haven't heard from U in ages!
U haven't 4gotten me, right? ☺
Hope UR good—
I'm Gr8!
K, not really cuz IM actually completely homesick!

Write back!
Colby
P.S. Say hi 2 Levi! PLZ!!

## CRUEL SUMMER

June 26

I was going to post a bunch of pictures of this name-day festival that Tally and Tassos dragged me to, but since apparently no one is even commenting on this blog, much less reading it, I'm not going to bother. I mean, what's the point?

But just so you know what you're missing, a name-day festival is actually a really big party that's held in honor of the Greeks who are named after saints (which, believe me, is practically all of them). And since just about every day of the year has been dedicated to the memory of a saint, they all celebrate their saint's day or "name-day" like they do a b-day, with roasted pigs and music and baklava (which is like a really bizarre dessert, super crusty and drenched in honey), along with other assorted delicacies.

And just in case you're wondering (though I know you probably aren't), for those unfortunate few who are not named after a saint, well, they still get to party on All Saints' Day, which is sometime after Greek Easter (yes, they even have their own separate Easter here).

Okay, well, I wish you all a warm, wonderful, and terribly exciting summer.

Because mine's turning out to be pretty much the opposite.

Colby

COLBY'S JOURNAL FOR DESPERATE TIMES WHEN SHE'S SO
DEPRESSED SHE REFUSES TO LEAVE HER ROOM

June 27

Here is a list of PEOPLE WHO SUCK and the VERY
VALID reasons why:

1) Amanda—Not only has she yet to respond to
   my last two e-mails, but she's also yet to leave a
   comment on my blog, which makes me think
   she hasn't even read it after that one time, and
   even then all she did was bug me about that
   picture of Petros, and make fun of his mustache, and ask me if I hooked up with him, and
   a whole lot of other rude nonsense like that.
   Which pretty much leads me to believe that
   she's not at all the friend I ~~thought~~ hoped she
   was.

2) Levi Bonham—No e-mail. No contact. No
   comment.

3) Penelope—I don't have to actually KNOW her
   to know how bad she sucks. That picture of
   her hanging all over Levi at that party I didn't
   get to go to (because I'm stuck HERE!) was
   worth a trillion, gazillion words.

4) <u>My mom</u>—Um, excuse me, but where to even begin?

5) <u>My dad</u>—Ditto.

6) <u>Tinos</u>—Yes I know Tinos is an island and not a person, but it's also not Mykonos, which means it sucks. Totally and completely sucks. Leave it to me to end up on the world's most boring island ever.

7) ~~Tally~~

8) ~~Tassos~~

Okay, the reason I crossed Tally and Tassos off the list is because I just realized that they don't actually suck. I mean, granted, they are a little weird, what with all their plant-whispering, meditating, hippie-music-loving stuff. But still, it's not like they really bug me all that bad or anything. Because the truth is, they pretty much leave me alone.

Like right now for instance, I've basically been holed up in my room for the last two days, and all Tally has done so far is stick her head in each morning and go, "Hey, no Internet café today?"

And I just shrug, sigh, roll my eyes, and stare at the ceiling some more.

And then she goes, "Okay, well, just so you know Tassos is heading out to his studio." (He's an artist, does marble sculptures and also makes ceramics and stuff. He's pretty good too, and kind of famous, at least in the world of marble sculpture and ceramics.) "And I'm heading to the shop, but we'll both be back around two in case you want to go to the beach. But if not, that's cool too."

And the funny thing is, she said all of that as though I haven't already memorized their schedules by now. I mean, every day it's pretty much the same thing—work in the morning, break at two for the beach, come home and eat a lunch made of whatever Tassos happened to catch and whatever's ripe in Tally's garden, then a quick shower before heading back to work for a few more hours, and then home for a late dinner where they usually invite a bunch of friends.

And even though it might sound like an okay life (I mean, if you really like to keep it simple, and back to basics, and enjoy a high tolerance for quiet moments with lots of boredom thrown in), and even though I sometimes relent and go to the beach with them, for the last two days, I've chosen not to.

I mean, what's the point?

What's the point of anything?

Because the fact is:

1) Amanda has moved on. Which means my senior year is destined to suck. Which means all my hard work was for nothing. Which means my shot at popularity is now null and void. Which means I'm back to being just another pathetic wannabe who fades into high school oblivion. Which means when I show up at my ten-year reunion everyone will go, "Colby? Colby <u>WHO</u>? Did you even go here?"

2) Levi forgot I exist. Because even though I stayed past my curfew, and even though I slept with him, I still refused to take off my dress. And because of that he's now moved on to some skinny strawberry-blond chick named Penelope who probably has no curfew and no problem with casual nudity. But the truth is, even if it wasn't Penelope it would still be someone else, because the cold hard fact is he never really liked me in the first place. He was just bored and restless and trying to pass the time. And even though I was never dumb enough to fool myself into thinking we were in love, or a couple, or anything remotely like that (mostly because I don't believe in any of that nonsense to begin with), still, you'd think he could at least take twenty seconds out of his extremely busy day to send me an e-mail, or something, since it's not like he didn't know I was a virgin.

3) My parents, who even though they cannot communicate about anything without yelling and screaming to the point where they've decided to communicate only through their attorneys, are apparently able to overcome their anger obstacles when it comes to all matters concerning me. Which means I was totally busted for my little letter-writing scam during the course of a very awkward, highly uncomfort-

able (um, that would be <u>ME</u> not <u>THEM,</u> as they were totally cool, calm, collected, and completely in the zone) ten-minute conference call where they informed me, in no uncertain terms, that I was to remain in Tinos, until my mandatory sentence has been completed, on the day otherwise known as August 31. And that there will be no time off for good behavior, bad behavior, or consideration of time served. And to stop trying to play them against each other because they're totally on to me.

So, in a nutshell, that is why I'm giving up.

I mean, I tried to make the best of it, I tried to keep in touch by creating a cute blog, sending e-mails, and writing letters and postcards so no one would forget me, but in the end, it just didn't work.

Because everyone did forget me.

Because they never really cared about me in the first place.

So rather than continue to beat my head against the wall, I've decided to spend the rest of my summer sitting right here in my little white room, emerging only for the occasional meal and bathroom break. I mean, if they want to put me in jail, then fine, I'll do the time.

But come August 31, I <u>WILL</u> be on that plane.

And I <u>WILL</u> return to Orange County.

Where my completely crummy life <u>WILL</u> still be waiting for me.

# CRUEL SUMMER

July 1

Okay, I know I said this blog was history since no one is reading it anyway, but the thing is, keeping this blog alive almost feels like it's keeping ME alive.

Seriously.

It's like, not only does it give me somewhere to go every day, but it also makes me feel like I have some kind of purpose.

Even if that purpose is just wasting my time, cribbing a blog that no one cares enough to read.

But since I'm actually kind of sick of just sitting in my room, I figured—*What the hey?* I'll just keep going.

Even if I am the only one who knows it exists.

Even if I am the only who cares.

So anyway, back to business:

1) This is a picture of my cat!

That's right, I adopted a kitten and he (or she, I haven't, um, really checked things out that thoroughly yet) is even more adorable in person. Seriously! Though I am really hoping it turns out to be a she because I named her/him/it Holly after Holly Golightly in *Breakfast at Tiffany's*. Partly because I totally love that movie/book, and partly because she's all black with a little white streak across her forehead—um, do cats have foreheads?

Whatever.

Anyway, she totally reminds me of Audrey Hepburn in the movie, because Audrey always dressed in those cute little black dresses, not to mention how she had a white streak too.

She was also really, really skinny, and when I found Holly she was really, really skinny too. And seemed like she needed protecting—just like Holly in both the book and movie versions!

The only thing is, I haven't actually told Tally and Tassos yet. Mostly because I know it probably wasn't the smartest thing to do since I'm leaving by the end of the summer anyway (YIPEE!!). But still, Holly was all alone when I found her (him?), just sitting in the middle of the dirt road, looking lost, and lonely and completely afraid. But the moment I knelt down, she ran right up and gazed at me with those big, sad, hungry blue eyes, and when she started rubbing against my leg and purring, well, obviously adoption was my only choice.

I mean, had I just left her there to fend for herself, there's a very good chance she never would've made it to the end of the day. But even if the best I can give her is a nice, happy, safe, and comfortable three months, then that may just be three more months than she otherwise would've gotten.

Besides, everything has a beginning, middle, and end. So when it's time to say good-bye, I'll be ready.

But for now, I totally plan to tell Tally and Tassos tonight—so wish me luck!

Even though I know I'm the only one reading this!
Colby

# CRUEL SUMMER

**Blog Comments:**

**Anonymous said:**

Good to see you are back to blogging again.
From someone who has read all of your posts.

**ColbyCat said:**

Mom, is this you???
I mean, I know it's you so just quit with the mysterious act. It's so dumb.

**Anonymous said:**

I'm definitely not your mom.
Though I'm sorry you think that I'm dumb.

**ColbyCat said:**

Um, okay. It's not that I think you're actually
dumb—whoever you are—it's just that I think the whole
ANONYMOUS thing is kind of—well—dumb.

**Anonymous said:**

Thank you for clearing that up. Though for now, I
still choose to remain ANONYMOUS, even though I
know you think that it's dumb.
P.S. I like your cat.

COLBY'S JOURNAL FOR DESPERATE TIMES FOR THINGS
SHE CAN'T POSSIBLY POST IN HER BLOG NOW THAT
SHE KNOWS MYSTERIOUS SOMEONE IS READING IT

July 2

Okay, I know it was only recently that I was whining and going on and on about how no one was reading my blog. Well now, apparently somebody is. Only I don't know who, since they signed in under ANONYMOUS. And even though I seriously considered restricting all anonymous comments, in the end I just couldn't do it. Mostly because it'd be like booting out your best (and only!) customer—not unlike what Petros often does to me.

And it's weird how I originally thought I wanted lots of readers and comments, but now I'm not so sure. I mean, now that I know someone is reading it, I'm no longer sure what to write. I guess if I knew WHO was reading it, then it might make it easier. Like, if it's my mom or dad, then I could use my blog for maximum effect, and make my life sound so lonely and pathetic they'd have to be completely inhuman (which I'm beginning to think they are) not to feel awful and guilty enough to let me come home.

But if it's Levi, then obviously the pathetic angle would be all wrong. I mean, I don't want to come off as ecstatic or anything (because then he might think that things are too good here, and that I actually don't need him to visit me—which would be so completely false!). But I don't want to sound quite so bored and depressed either.

I guess the perfect balance is to sound a little bored, but only because I'm just way too cool to even be here in the first place. (Thus making my blog an experiment in fiction!)

And if it's Amanda, then I definitely need to make it sound like I'm totally partying and hanging with the cool group, so she won't start regretting that she ever started talking to me in the first place (even though she probably/ obviously does).

See how complicated this has become now that I have a subscriber?

I swear, it was a whole lot easier when I was the only reader.

On another note, Tally and Tassos are totally cool with Holly. In fact, not only do they think she's totally adorable, but Tally has kind of taken over the care and maintenance of her, buying her a collar and a litter box and feeding her some organic stuff that's supposed to build a better kitty. And even though I'm really happy and relieved that they love her, at the same time all of that kindness and support makes me feel pretty bad about not telling them sooner. I mean, coming home from the café only to find Tally down on her hands and knees, wiping a puddle of cat pee from the floor definitely was not the best way to introduce our latest addition.

But still, I guess it all worked out in the end, and they're totally on board with keeping the name Holly, even though we recently discovered that she is actually a HE.

So because of all that, I've decided to make more of an effort to go to the beach, pitch in, and hang out with them. I mean, they were so cool about Holly, and just about everything else I've dumped on them, like my endless moping, silent treatment, and mood swings, that I kind of feel obligated to at least pretend like I'm having some fun (even though I'm not).

I guess I'm also starting to realize just how much I'm actually intruding on them, what a huge imposition I am. I mean, here my aunt moved all the way across the ocean to some tiny, obscure Greek island, probably for the sole purpose of getting away from everything, including my mom, my dad, my grandma, and me, only to get stuck with me for almost three months.

I mean, even though their life may be a little too <u>ORGANIC</u> for my tastes, a little too <u>SLOW, LOW ON EXCITEMENT,</u> and definitely <u>NOTHING</u> I'd ever choose for myself, obviously it works for them.

And just as they have it all worked out, and are firmly entrenched in their happy place, I show up, and pretty much pout, slam doors, barely talk for weeks on end, and then top it all off by dragging home a stray cat that likes to pee on the floor.

And while I'm on the subject (of Tally, not cat pee), let me just say that I'm also kind of annoyed by how my parents always used to make fun of her. I mean, okay, so she's a little quirky, and granted she's definitely more than a little weird in some ways, but really, what's the big deal?

Because she's also really nice, and generous, and understanding, and kind, not to mention how she opened her door to me when my parents closed theirs. And from the first day on she made it clear that she's there for me if I need her, but that she'll stay out of my way if I don't. And the only rule of the house is that we respect each other as well as ourselves.

That's it!

No curfew.

No chores.

No rules for the sake of having rules.

So yeah, maybe she is the opposite of my parents, but I'm beginning to think that's not such a bad thing . . .

Anyway, tomorrow, Tassos is supposed to show me how to catch an octopus with my bare hands! Apparently this is quite difficult to master, even though he makes it look easy. But I'm thinking I might just stick with swimming behind and holding the bag, because I've gotten pretty good at that. And I'm not so sure I need to add Experienced Octopus Catcher to my resume.

## CRUEL SUMMER

July 4

So apparently the Greeks don't celebrate the Fourth of July. And even though you're probably thinking—duh!—let me just explain how it's always been my favorite holiday, which means BBQs and fireworks have been such a big, important part of every single one of my summers, for as far back as I can remember, that it feels really weird (and sad) not to be celebrating it in the same way today.

Though before you go thinking I'm a completely clueless dork, let me just explain that I really do get why the Greeks don't exactly care about our independence from the Brits. Though understanding their reasons doesn't do much to lessen my current case of extreme homesickness. Because I can only imagine all of the awesome beach and backyard BBQs that my friends are all going to, and that I'm totally missing out on. Not to mention how I always used to buy a new bikini, flip-flops, and cover-up to wear to those parties, but after checking out the shops here, and seeing how they're stocked with totally lame merchandise, that's so <u>NOT</u> going to happen!

But still, Tally and Tassos are planning to leave work early so they can throw a big party. And, I admit, when they first told me about it, I thought they were doing it for my benefit, so of course I was all—*oh, you don't have to, blah, blah, blah*. But they just laughed and explained how they do it every year as my aunt is not the only American living here (yup, there are a few other crazies as well!) so they're going to invite a bunch of friends over to BBQ and celebrate, though they did warn me there won't be any fireworks.

Anyway, I should probably get back and help them set up, but to anyone back home who might actually be reading this—Happy Fourth!

Colby

July 4
To: AmandaStar
From: ColbyCat
Re: 4th!

I haven't heard from U 4ever, so I hope UR good. Also, Happy 4th. I no UR prbly going 2 the beach or a party or somethun so have fun!

E-mail me! (When U can)
~Colby
P.S. Any news on Levi? Lemme no!


COLBY'S JOURNAL FOR DESPERATE TIMES
WHEN THINGS TAKE AN ASTONISHING, SURPRISING,
UNEXPECTED TURN FOR THE BETTER

July 5

After one and a half glasses of homemade Greek wine and several test sips of ouzo on the rocks (each sip was just to make sure it was really as bad as I thought), I admit, this is probably not the best time to be writing about this, or anything else for that matter, but I'm afraid if I wait until morning then I won't remember a thing, so here goes:

I HAD FUN.

Shocking but serious. And it's not like I was expecting it, or even thought it was in any way remotely possible, but still, there you have it.

I mean, it's not like I thought it would be awful or

anything, and I guess there was a small part of me that was actually kind of looking forward to it, but still, it's not like I have any friends of my own here, so I pretty much thought I'd be stuck with a bunch of adults, listening to old music and stuff.

And even though it did kind of turn out like that, I somehow managed to have fun in spite of it. And only twice (okay, maybe thrice) did I compare it unfavorably to the Fourth of July parties back home. Though that's only because there were no fireworks—or at least not the kind you shoot into the sky!

Though there was another kind of fireworks.

The kind that explode in your chest.

And here's why:

### I MET SOMEONE.

Not so earth shattering, I know, since the only people I knew to begin with were Tally and Tassos and a few of their friends, which still left quite a few other people to meet. But in this case what I mean is, I met someone ~~special~~.

Okay, I just reread that and it looks totally dorky and lame. So let me just rephrase it and say I met this really cute guy, who smiled at me from across the backyard for like two full hours before he finally came over to talk to me.

And when he did, this is what he said: "Ya'Sou, I'm Yannis." Followed by a big smile.

So I went: "Hey, I'm Colby. Your friend almost ran me over with his Vespa." And then I started laughing. And then, luckily, he started laughing too.

And then he said, "I saw you crying on the boat."

Which, to be honest, was actually really embarrassing. But still, I just laughed, partly because I WAS crying on the boat so it's not like I could go back and erase it, but mostly because he's so unbelievably cute, and has such a nice smile, I didn't really know what else to do.

Anyway, did I mention he was cute? Well, this is what he looks like:

1) Dark, wavy hair—almost, but not quite black, that on anyone else I would say he needs a haircut, but on him, that longish, messy look is totally smokin'.

2) Really nice tan.

3) Piercing green eyes (seriously, like, see-straight-through-to-your-soul kind of eyes).

4) Very thick eyelashes—the kind that are usually only provided courtesy of Maybelline.

5) Nice eyebrows, with the ability to raise only one (I've tried, but I've never been able to do that), which, by the way, is extremely sexy.

6) Amazingly hot bod—lean, muscled, and neither too tall nor too short, but just exactly right.

7) Nice, friendly smile with slightly crooked front teeth, which doesn't bother me as much as I would've thought, since it just makes him kind of quirky and even that much cuter.

8) Decent English language skills, with a supercute,

definitely sexy accent. (And even though I realize that doesn't exactly qualify as part of his appearance, I still think it's worth mentioning.)

9) Um, did I mention his amazingly hot body? I did? Oh, well, I guess it's just so amazing it's worth mentioning twice!

Okay, so anyway, after we laughed (at my expense) we both just kind of stood there looking at each other in the most uncomfortable, awkward way. And it seemed like it dragged on forever, to the point where I actually thought I heard the small hand on my watch timing me to see just how long I could sustain an embarrassing pause—but then I was even more embarrassed when I realized it was actually the sound of my own rapidly beating heart crashing against my chest!

Seriously!

Well, kind of.

Anyway, so then these two girls who looked to be somewhere around my age, walked right up, looked at me briefly, and then turned to Yannis and said something that I totally could not understand (but that made me realize I should probably stop being so resistant to change and start trying to learn Greek, *pronto*).

And then he looked at me and said, "It was nice meeting you."

And then they pulled him away. And I mean LITER-ALLY pulled him away, like, with one on each arm, all the way to the opposite side of the yard, which was pretty much as far from me as you could possibly get.

And even though the pulling him away part could definitely be considered the low point of the night, luckily, it didn't end there. Because later, much later, when it was dark, and a lot of the adults were pretty tipsy from all that organic homemade wine they were drinking, Tassos put on a Greek CD and everyone started dancing. Only not the kind of dancing like I'm used to, but instead they were all holding hands and kind of like running in a circle. So I just sat there, with Holly on my lap, sipping from the small glass of ouzo Tassos gave me to try, fighting the overwhelming urge to gag and vomit (I mean, it's seriously AWFUL), when everyone was like, "Hey Colby, come join us!"

But I just shook my head, determined to stay put since I don't exactly know any of those dance moves, and no way was I going to risk looking like a big, clumsy dork in front of SUPERHOT YANNIS. Not to mention how those two Greek girls were totally staring at me in a way that made it pretty obvious just how much they'd LOVE to watch me do a face plant right in front of them.

But then Yannis broke away from the circle, grabbed my hand, and pulled me into the group. And even though I probably looked like a fool, it wasn't all that long before I was too busy laughing and enjoying myself (especially the way my hand felt in his!) to even think about how dumb I appeared.

And then we pretty much danced for the rest of the

night, or at least until Tassos cut the music and made everyone go home.

And even though all we did was hold hands, and even though it was only because the dance required it, the way he looked at me when he said good-bye, was (almost) as good as any kiss I've ever had.

Okay, well, it's almost three now and I can barely keep my eyes open so—

*Kalinichta!*

(That means good night in Greek!)

## CRUEL SUMMER

July 5

Who said the Greeks don't know how to celebrate the Fourth of July?

Certainly not me!

Granted, there were no fireworks, but that doesn't mean it wasn't fun—and if you don't believe me, then see for yourself:

1) That's me eating a mongo huge piece of watermelon. I swear, the fruit here is so much sweeter than the fruit you get at home. Seriously, it tastes like a million times better, and I just can't get enough. Oh yeah, notice the deep, dark tan I'm sporting, and the blond streaks in my hair? Believe it or not, that's after <u>JUST A FEW DAYS</u> at the beach. It's like, even the sun's rays are sweeter here too!

2) That's Mr. Holly Golightly, sitting on a chair, observing all the action. He can be a little aloof at times, and would rather watch than join in.

3) That's Tassos roasting a lamb. And yes, believe it or not, they roast the whole dang thing. They eat the whole dang thing too. I'm not kidding. They eat the brains, the liver, the tongue—EVERYTHING! Nothing goes to waste. And yes, I'm well aware of how sad, not to mention how completely creepy it looks, seeing it all skinned like that, but trust me, after awhile you get pretty desensitized to that stuff. I mean, that very same morning when I opened the fridge in the shed and saw that same exact lamb all hairless, bent in half, and awkwardly shoved in there, I didn't even scream! Though I did the first time I saw something like that. As well as the second.

4) That's everybody dancing—Greek dancing, which is pretty much a group activity as you can see.

5) That's me dancing!

6) That's all!

July 6
To: NatalieZee
From: ColbyCat
Re: You're moving?
Hey Nat,

In answer to your e-mail regarding the FOR SALE sign you

saw in my yard—let me just say that it's all a big misunder-standing. Though I thank you for your concern.

You're probably surprised to see me answering you back. Especially after that whole thing with Amanda and how you accused me of "selling out" so I could be "popular, shallow, and a big conforming retard."

That IS how you put it, right Nat?

And yet, here I am, not only answering you back, but also using proper English and spelling, as I know how much you hate all of those e-mail/text message shortcuts.

Still think I'm shallow?

Anyway, you're probably not even aware of this since we haven't talked for months, but I'm currently in Greece, where I'm spending the summer on the island of Tinos with my aunt Tally (and no, she's not really crazy, my parents were just joking), so I probably won't be writing you back anytime soon, since I'm super busy going to the beach and hanging in clubs with all of the really good friends I've made here.

Also, you'll never believe this but LEVI BONHAM is to-tally coming to visit! Seriously, I forget exactly when, but the point is that he'll be here soon! That's because we pretty much spent my whole last night together, so now he's plan-ning to get on a cruise ship so he can come see me! I guess he misses me, or something.

Anyway, thanks for the heads-up, but it's not at all what you think. I'm DEFINITELY not moving.

Well, take care—

Colby

*July 7*

*Dear Mom,*

<u>*THE HOUSE IS FOR SALE???*</u>

*Exactly how long did you think you could keep this from me? Because for your information I still have plenty of friends back home who report to me on a regular basis, one of whom informed me that <u>THE HOUSE IS FOR SALE!</u>*

*And since I know this <u>CANNOT</u> be happening, I'd really appreciate it if you could write me back immediately, or better yet— I'm going to call you, since we obviously have a lot to discuss.*

*Love,*

*Your soon to be homeless daughter who is <u>SHOCKED</u> and <u>DISMAYED</u> by the way her parents are gambling with her future,*

*Colby*


*July 7*

*Dear Dad,*

*It has come to my attention that my childhood home is now featuring a FOR SALE sign on the front lawn, and I'm hoping you can shed some light on the subject.*

*I've spoken to Mom on the phone, and according to her, this is mostly your doing. She said it's all part of the divorce settlement, because you wanted to cash in and divide the money evenly.*

*But here's something you may not have considered:*

<u>*WHAT'S IN IT FOR ME?*</u>

*I mean, while it's all fine and good for you to split the proceeds and move to opposite ends of the earth, did you ever <u>STOP,</u> take a deep breath, and ask yourself—*

*HEY, WHAT ABOUT COLBY?*
*You remember, YOUR DAUGHTER, Colby?*
*The one you BANISHED to Greece?*
*Just how might she feel about this? How might this affect HER?*

Because I'm starting to think that neither you nor Mom even thought to consider me, at any time, during your hectic, illogical, decision-making process.

Though maybe you should have.

I mean, just because you guys decided to move on, doesn't mean I'm in on it too. Did it ever occur to you that maybe I don't want to move on? Did you ever *STOP* and consider *THAT?*

Because, truth be told, Dad, I actually *LIKE* living in my comfortable home, in my nice neighborhood, that's within walking distance to my school and all of my friends' houses. I used to feel good, *SAFE EVEN,* just knowing I had two parents to come home to. Not to mention a roof over my head.

Because now, according to Mom, once the house is sold, we will no longer be able to afford to live in Orange County, and may even have to move *OUT OF STATE!* She even mentioned something about going to *ARIZONA!* And maybe you're not aware of this, but I don't know *ANYONE* in Arizona! All I know about Arizona is that it's one hundred and twenty degrees *IN THE SHADE!* Which, you've got to admit, is not exactly a selling point.

So I strongly urge you both to reconsider, before it's too late to reverse all the damage you've set in motion.

As for me, all I can do now is sit back and helplessly watch while the two of you do your very best to destroy my life as I once knew it.

Love,

*Your completely depressed, but not like you care, daughter—*
*Colby*

July 8
To: AmandaStar
From: ColbyCat
Re: I need a favor
Hey Amanda,

Um, I no U must B really busy & all since U haven't written me back in a really long time, but I'm Idering if U could do me a favor? Next time UR driving by my house, maybe U could stop long enuff 2 remove the 4 Sale sign on my front lawn? Bcuz I'd really appreciate it.

U can just stick it in UR trunk, or a nearby trash can, or whatever.

Thanks,

Colby

P.S. Um, any news on Levi & if he's still going on that cruise? Lemme know, bcuz I still haven't heard from him & IV been Idering!?

Write back, plz!

## Colby's Journal for Desperate Times
### When Life Becomes a Roller Coaster That
### Will Not Stop or Slow Down

July 8

I don't get it. I seriously do not get it. I mean, first I'm totally hating my life, and am more than happy to focus on the bad things—which admittedly, is pretty much every-thing here. But then one day, I wake up, take a look around, and decide to stop fighting it, decide to stop acting like such a big whiny loser, and start participating around the house (mostly because time goes by faster when you're busy) and try to show a little gratitude toward Tally and Tassos so they won't think I'm a complete and total burden.

And then, shortly after that, I meet a completely dreamy local named Yannis, who almost makes me forget about Levi, and who also, at least from what I could tell, seemed to like me too.

And I'm thinking—yipee!

Things are finally looking up!

Maybe it's true what Tally and Tassos always say—that happy attracts happy—or however they put it.

But then, just as I'm starting to smile again, I get an e-mail from Natalie Zippenhoffer, my former best friend since second grade turned girl I no longer talk to much less acknowledge. And she's all too happy to inform me that my HOUSE IS FOR SALE!

Okay, to be fair, I don't really know that she was happy. Because there's a part of me that thinks she might've just been concerned, which, if that's the case, then I feel even worse for way too many reasons to mention.

But what I do know is this:

One moment I was riding high!

And the next I'm completely homeless.

And trust me, that is not an exaggeration, because the

fact is not only has my mom recently exhibited some very bad decision-making skills, but when I asked her just what she had in mind for us after the sale, just where she envisioned the two of us living—she answered with a verbal shrug. Which basically amounted to a couple of *ums,* followed by some throat clearing and *we'll sees,* along with a bunch of statistical nonsense about median home prices in Orange County, mortgage rates, and *blah, blah, blah.* All of which pretty much translates to—*Gee, Colby, I don't really know what will become of you. I hadn't really thought about it until you just now brought it up!*

And then just as I thought it couldn't get any worse, she tosses something in there about moving to <u>ARIZONA</u>! Just dropped it right in there, as though I wouldn't even notice.

And just for the record, <u>I AM NOT MOVING TO ARIZONA!</u>

There's just no way.

I <u>WON'T</u> do it.

She <u>CANNOT</u> make me.

And as for Yannis? Well, I haven't seen or heard from him since the Fourth of July party, which means I am an even worse judge of these things than I thought, because I really was convinced that he just might kinda like me. But then again, when I think back on the colossal mistake I made with Levi (which is pretty much all the time since I really can't stop thinking about it, even though I truly wish I could), I guess I shouldn't be all that surprised.

All I really know for sure is that this "happy gets happy" nonsense is a total crock of crap.

# CRUEL SUMMER

**Blog Comments:**

**Anonymous said:**

Why do you call it Cruel Summer?
Do you really hate Tinos that much?
From someone who cares.

**ColbyCat said:**

It's after a song from the eighties, by some all-girl band called Bananarama. But you already knew that since your mom used to play it when she cleaned the house.

Yes, I know this is <u>YOU,</u> Natalie. So why don't you just come clean and show yourself already! This is so freaking lame.

**Anonymous said:**

I'm definitely not Natalie, though her mom sounds cool!

Maybe you should stop blogging so much and get out more. You might have more fun.
Just a thought.

Sorry you think I am both dumb and lame.

**ColbyCat Said:**

<u>"GET OUT MORE"?</u>
I should've known it was <u>YOU,</u> Petros.

So allow me to remind you that I am your VERY BEST customer, and without me, where would you be?

Maybe you should spend your next siesta trying to sharpen your customer service skills.

Seriously. Please think about it. It really couldn't hurt.

**Anonymous said:**

No, I'm definitely not Petros either.

Who's Petros?

Should I be jealous?

COLBY'S JOURNAL FOR DESPERATE TIMES WHEN LIFE BECOMES SO UNBELIEVABLY GOOD AGAIN SHE CAN'T POSSIBLY PUT IT IN HER BLOG

July 9

OMG—I now know who ANONYMOUS is!

It's Levi Bonham!

!!!!!!!!!!!!!!!!!!!!!!!!!!!!!

I mean, who else could it be?

Obviously he hasn't written or e-mailed because he's too busy playing blog comment games, trying to figure out if I've met someone he should be jealous of! Which means he didn't forget me! Which also means I can stop torturing myself for making a huge error in judgment, because obviously, I didn't!

And even though I know it sounds crazy and delusional, here's the proof:

1) It's not Natalie because she's too honest, too straightforward, too in-your-face to play games like that.
2) It's not my mom because she doesn't even know how to turn the computer on much less post a comment.
3) It's not Amanda because she can't even be bothered to e-mail me back much less comment on my blog. Besides, that kind of blog banter just isn't her thing.
4) It's not my dad because he's too annoyed with me and my letters to actually take the time to joke around with me.
5) It's not anyone in Tinos because the only one who even knows about my blog is Petros and his English is pretty limited. And Tally and Tassos don't even have access to a computer.
6) So basically, the only possibility left is Levi! And even though he can't really carry on a conversation in person, I'm willing to bet that like most people, he's better on paper (or in this case, on screen).

But before I make my next move (or, um, post), I have to think very carefully about how to proceed.

I mean, I could:

1) Continue as usual, blogging about all the usual, boring, mundane things I do here, acting as

though I have no idea that <u>LEVI BONHAM IS READING MY BLOG.</u> And then, each time he decides to leave a comment, I'll pretend like I think it's just about everyone <u>BUT</u> him, until he eventually gives up and reveals himself, then we can both enjoy a good laugh about it when he comes to visit me on his cruise!

2) I lie. Which basically means I start blogging about a life that's a whole lot better than the one I'm actually living. And then, when he comments, I pretend like I think he's just one of the many gorgeous, hot Greek guys that are lining up to go out with me. Though I have to be careful to not overdo it and keep it believable. I mean just because I'm far away doesn't mean anyone's gonna believe I suddenly turned into Amanda.

3) I act confident and forthright (which is pretty much the opposite of me) and the next time he comments, I write a reply like, "Hey Levi! Let me know when you're heading off on that cruise so I can <u>TRY</u> to meet up with you!" Though obviously I won't put the "try" part in all caps. But still, he'll get the gist.

And after reviewing all three choices, I think I'll go with #2. Basically because it's going to be way too hard for me to try to pull off #3, and I don't really want to take the

#1 approach and keep up my loser blog either, because actually, well, it's a little depressing. So obviously that leaves me with #2.

Besides, what could it hurt to make my life sound a little better than it is?

## **VERY RECENT UPDATE**
### (Technically July 10)

There's more!

OMG—get this! Right after dinner I went to my room, and I was barely in there two seconds when Tally knocked on my door and said, "Yannis is here."

And even though I had this immediate flash of his image in my mind, even though I knew exactly who she meant, I also thought it would be a good opportunity to try out my cool, new blog persona. So I narrowed my eyes and tried to look confused as I said, "Who?"

But I guess Tally's too smart for that, because she just shook her head and laughed and said, "Go on, he's waiting out front."

So I scooped Holly off my bed, peered into the mirror and ran my hands through my hair real quick, trying to fluff it up and make it look tousled and cute as opposed to flat and limp, then I went outside to where Yannis was sitting on his Vespa, looking just as cute (maybe even cuter!) as he did on the Fourth of July. And it was so amazing to see him sitting there like that, especially since I'd convinced myself I'd never see him again.

I hugged Holly tightly to my chest, watching as Yannis smiled in a way that showcased the dimples on either side of his cheeks, as his deep green eyes gazed into mine. Though I guess it was a little too close for Holly because he immediately started protesting, and squirming, and scratching at me to get away.

"So what's up?" I asked, setting Holly down and watching as he scrammed back inside the house, but not before leaving a burning red spot on my arm, where his claws nearly broke through my skin.

"I was wondering if you want to go for a ride?" Yannis asked, his gaze still on mine.

And it wasn't until I'd climbed on the back of his bike and wrapped my arms tightly around his waist, that I realized I'd forgotten to ask where.

But as it turned out, we ended up in town, at a club that seemed like it was filled with all of his family and friends.

"Have you been here before?" he asked, grabbing my hand and pulling me inside.

So of course, still trying to come off as cool, experienced, and worldly, I just shrugged and said, "Um, maybe. I really can't remember." And then I gazed down at my khaki shorts and black tank top and wished I'd at least taken the time to change before I agreed to go out with him.

But he just smiled, and said, "My cousin owns it." Then he proceeded to introduce me to like one hundred and thirty different people who all seemed to be somehow related.

"So is everyone on this island your cousin?" I asked,

no longer trying to keep all the names straight, and just nodding and smiling instead.

But he just laughed and said, "No, it only seems that way."

Then he pulled me out to the dance floor, where we stayed for most of the night. Only this time it was regular, modern dancing as opposed to that traditional, running-in-a-circle Greek dancing. Which also means I didn't have an excuse to hold his hand. But still, it was pretty cool just to hang out in a club, and enjoy a cocktail or two, and be treated like an adult for a change. Even though we didn't actually have any cocktails and just ordered two Cokes instead. But still, it's the KNOWING that you can have whatever you want that makes it so great.

Though I guess Yannis is probably pretty used to stuff like that since he grew up here and all. Well, both here and in Athens, since, as he told me, his family only comes here for the summers (which is why I saw him on the boat, he was coming back for the summer) and then he returns to Athens for school. Which actually seems like a pretty cool life. Except for the fact that he probably won't be here next summer because he's in his last year of high school and after that he has to go into the military for at least a year.

That's exactly what he said—HAS TO.

Like, no choice whatsoever.

Apparently the only choice he has in the matter is WHEN. Like, he can go right after high school, or right after college, or even put it off until he's in his forties. But in the end, he HAS to go. No exceptions. Which seems like it would really suck, but he didn't seem all that bothered by it.

So at one point, we were sitting in a booth, taking a break, when they started playing some traditional Greek song. And right out of nowhere (or at least it seemed that way to me) one of those girls from the Fourth of July party walked up, gave me a quick, sharp, not so nice once-over, then turned to Yannis and said something in Greek that, from what I could guess, was the equivalent of asking him to dance.

Seriously! Right in front of me! And even though it seemed really weird, I mean considering how we were obviously enjoying ourselves and not looking for any kind of distraction, it's not like I could do anything about it, since it's not like we're a couple.

I glanced back and forth between them, wondering what Yannis would do, my heart thumping hard in my chest as he smiled, shook his head, and stayed seated.

And then, just like in a movie, she narrowed her kohl-lined eyes on mine, tossed her long black hair over her shoulder, and marched across the room, all the way to the other side where her friend from the Fourth of July BBQ, the one with the botched dye job that left her hair an unfortunate shade of tangerine, stood glaring at me.

So then I looked at Yannis and went, "Um, who was that? Another cousin?" And then I laughed—though it was definitely more of a nervous laugh than a real laugh, but the moment was so awkward and tense I didn't really know what to do.

But he just shook his head and shrugged. Then he got

up to get us more Cokes, and by the time he came back, we moved on to something else, and I pretty much forgot all about it 'til now.

When the club was closing and it was time to leave, I climbed on the back of his bike, wrapped my arms around his waist, and buried my face in his neck, closing my eyes to the passing scenery, the full moon, the chilled air—losing myself in the warmth of his body and the way he managed to smell so good without the aid of cologne or aftershave or anything remotely artificial.

But by the time we made it back to my house, I suddenly felt so awkward, and funny, and nervous, and weird, I just hopped off the back and bolted for the door. And just when I realized I hadn't said thanks, much less good night, he called, "Hey, you forgot something."

I gazed down at myself, taking inventory of my shorts, my tank top, my flip-flops, seeing everything still present and accounted for, and wondering what he meant. But when I looked up again, he was waving at me to come closer, and I knew it was all just a ploy, some silly ruse so he could try and make a move.

But instead, he just reached inside his pocket and retrieved the silver Tiffany's bracelet I'd lost while we were dancing, the one I'd forgotten all about until it was dangling right before me.

So I offered my arm and held my breath, watching as his fingers brushed across the thin blue lines on my wrist, feeling the clasp snap shut, and becoming so dizzy and breathless I thought I might faint.

And when I looked at him again, I knew he was going to kiss me. And just as I was about to close my eyes and lean in, he smiled, mumbled something in Greek I couldn't even begin to understand, then started his bike and rode away.

The second he was gone, I ran for the door, repeating the phrase over and over, anxious for either Tally or Tassos to translate. But when I got inside, they were already asleep, and by the time I got to my room, and grabbed this journal, the words had disappeared.

*July 10*

*Dear Tally and/or Tassos,*

*I __MUST__ learn Greek! Immediately! And you can help me by __ONLY__ communicating with me in Greek from now on.*

*I'm serious.*

*This means that even when you're talking to each other and I happen to walk in the room, it would really help if you could immediately switch your conversation to Greek.*

*This is what they call the Immersion Method.*

*This is how my Spanish teacher does it.*

*And this is why I got an A in Spanish III last semester.*

*Also, I need to ask you about these two girls that were here on the Fourth of July that I think you might know. One has long black hair, and the other has this kind of orangey colored hair (like she tried for blond but only made it halfway). Anyway, anything you can tell me about them would be greatly appreciated. Though I'm afraid this particular conversation will have to be in English, as I need to understand every word.*

Okay, I'm heading into town to hang at the café for the rest of the day.

So—have fun at the beach!

Love,

Colby

July 11

Dear Dad,

Even though I just got off the phone with you, I realize there are still a few important things I didn't get a chance to say, so I will write them down here.

1) I don't think it's at all fair for you to say that there are things that happen between adults that I cannot possibly understand. Because I <u>DO</u> understand, Dad—more than you can possibly know. It's <u>YOU</u> who never tries to understand <u>ME.</u>

2) If Mom and I have to move to <u>ARIZONA</u> then when will I get to see you? Did you ever think of that? Because it's a whole other state, which means joint custody and alternate weekends are pretty much out of the question.

3) The last time I spoke to Mom, she informed me that you have a new girlfriend. And even though I waited through our entire phone call for you to mention her, you never once did. And just as I was about to take the plunge and ask you myself, it seemed like you somehow sensed it and that's why you claimed you had a call on another line. So don't go thinking I was fooled, because I wasn't.

Anyway, I'd really appreciate it if you could write me back at your earliest convenience, as I'm obviously in need of some answers.

Or if you're too busy to write, then maybe you can just send me a plane ticket so I can fly home and we can hash it out in person.

Seriously, Dad, this is no laughing matter.

Love,

Colby

July 11

Dear Mom,

Yes, I talked to Dad on the phone, and no, I didn't learn anything about his new girlfriend because he faked another call and hung up before I got a chance to ask. Though to be honest, I'm really not so sure I want to talk about it anyway. I mean, it's really kind of inappropriate, not to mention creepy.

Because the truth is, if anyone in this family should be dating—it's ME!

I'M the teenager.

I'M the one who's supposed to be single.

And I really hate to break it to you, but you and Dad already had your chance, you already got your shot at being sweet sixteen, so it seems pretty unfair that you pick NOW to attempt to do it again.

You don't get to be a teenager twice, Mom. It's just not right.

And by the way things are going, I'm sure it's just a matter of time before YOU decide to hook up too, so I'd like to make it clear, right from the start, that I'm really not interested in hearing any of the gory details.

Because the truth is, I'm just not up for any of this.

Probably because I didn't ASK for any of this.

And excuse me for saying so, but in light of recent events, I just can't help but think that the only reason you guys sent me away to begin with is so you could be free to date, and party, and basically enjoy all of the things that I should be enjoying, only I'm NOT, because YOU sent me HERE!

Which is so completely wrong on so many levels.

Ask your shrink, I'm sure she'll agree.

Love,

The Completely Desperate and Absolutely Serious,

Colby

P.S. I'm enclosing a picture of this famous church here called the *Panagia Evangelistria* where the Virgin Mary is said to appear, or where they found an old famous icon of her, or something like that (okay, I don't really know the history, but that's not really the point). The point is that every year ~~hundreds~~ no, make that THOUSANDS of religious pilgrims crawl on their hands and knees all the way from the port to the church (which, trust me, is pretty dang far if you're crawling), just so they can pray. And even though I've yet to visit, I'm thinking I might go there today . . . because as you can see, I'm running out of options, and am desperately in need of a MIRACLE.

July 11
To: AmandaStar
From: ColbyCat
Re: Thx anyway
Hey Amanda,

Good 2 finally hear from U & no, I guess I really didn't stop 2 think about how your trunk would be so full of shopping bags there wouldn't B any room left 4 the 4 Sale sign.

Tho I'm glad 2 hear UR having fun. Those pics of U and Jenna and her cousin Penelope (I didn't no she had a cousin? I also didn't no U & Jenna were friends again? When did that happen? Bcuz last I heard you sed U H8D her) at Fashion Island were v cute.

Things R better here, I've made a ton of friends & I'm kinda c-ing someone. But if Levi still wants 2 come, I'm sure I can make room!☺

In fact, don't even mention it 2 him—K?

TTYL—

Colby

July 11
To: NatalieZee
From: ColbyCat
Re: You're moving?
Hey Nat—

While I'm not really sure why the FOR SALE sign is still on my lawn, at this point it's really between my mom and my dad, since, like I wrote in my last e-mail to you, I'm spending the summer in Greece and I'm far too busy having fun here to worry about anything that's going on back home.

And while I truly appreciate your concern, you really don't need to continue to update me.

Though if you do feel like directing your concerns to either one of my parents, or, better yet, stopping by my house and getting rid of the sign yourself—that would be fine.

Hope you're enjoying the summer.
Take care,
Colby

## CIRCLE IN THE SAND
## (FORMERLY CRUEL SUMMER)

July 14

Since someone who goes by the name of ANONY-MOUS recently accused me of hating Tinos because of the name of this blog, I've decided to change it. Which shouldn't be at all confusing since no one but ANONY-MOUS is reading it anyway, and I'm assuming he/she/they have it bookmarked already.

Anyway, it's funny because this is also named after a song my friend's (well, former friend's) mom used to sing all the time—I guess she was really big on songs about summer.

So I hope, ANONYMOUS, whoever you are, that you'll happen to agree that this title is much more neutral, and far less negative, though probably still not quite as upbeat as you were hoping.

Though maybe I should've titled it <u>CIRCLE IN THE DIRT</u>, because as you've probably noticed in the photos I've posted, there is no shortage of dirt in this place. Also, I recently learned that the Cyclades (which is what they call the group of islands that Tinos is part of) is actually ancient Greek for the word "Circle," so that seems pretty appropriate too. Not to mention how circles are continuous and have no end, and that's pretty much how this summer is beginning to feel—like an eternal loop of continuous days with no end in sight.

Though I'm hoping you won't read too much into what I just wrote and take it all wrong, because I guess what I'm really trying to say is that while I don't exactly hate it here anymore, if I was given the choice, I'd still rather not be here at all.

Though things might just be looking up, since just a second ago, Petros actually smiled and brought me a Nescafé Frappe—

ON THE HOUSE!

Maybe it's because I finally got a tan.

Maybe it's because I haven't been around the last few days since I've been so busy going to clubs, the beach, and hanging out with all my friends here, which gave him plenty of time to ruminate on the fact of just how much he needs me, and misses me, since I am his very best customer. But whatever the reason—just know this—it's really not as bad here as I once thought. But that doesn't mean that it's paradise either. It just means that it's no longer the opposite of paradise.

And now, for your viewing pleasure:

1) This is a picture (uploaded from a Web site since I didn't have my camera at the time) from a club I went to the other night with a friend. And just so you know, there are no age limits here, no I.D.

checks, no bouncers, no velvet ropes, no rules, no nonsense. Just equal-opportunity good times for all ages! Viva Tinos!

2) This is a picture of the scratch Holly Golightly made on my arm that very same night, right before I went to the club. Though it's actually not nearly as bad as it looks, and it really wasn't his fault since I held him too tight and I should know by now just how much he hates that. But still, it hurt like you cannot believe.

3) This is a picture of my aunt Tally and her boyfriend, Tassos, eating some sea urchin he caught at the beach. Seriously, they just pulled them right out of the water, cracked them right open (they have this special tool made just for that specific purpose), then they each grabbed a seashell and used it like a spoon to scoop out the insides, and I watched (and photographed) while they ate it RAW! I admit, I tried a little teensy bit too, but only because they're always telling me how it's good to keep an open mind and try new things. But even though I wouldn't exactly say that I loved it (because I definitely did NOT), I also have to admit that it wasn't nearly as gross as you're probably thinking! Though it definitely was a little bit gross!

4) This is a picture of Agios Fokas, which is the beach I'm heading to now, for the sole purpose of working on my tan, so I can maybe get another free frappe tomorrow!

Have a good day!

Love,

Colby

July 15

To: NatalieZee

From: ColbyCat

Re: You're moving

Thank you for trying to get rid of that stupid FOR SALE sign.

I really do appreciate it.

Though I have no idea why they've already replaced it with another.

But still, thanks for trying.

Colby

COLBY'S JOURNAL FOR DESPERATE TIMES WHEN SHE JUST
CAN'T UNDERSTAND ANYTHING ABOUT HER LIFE

July 16

This is how desperate I am—I actually flipped through one of Tally's New Age, self-empowerment, or whatever you call them books, searching for answers to my current predicament, and even <u>THEY</u> couldn't help.

Though that's probably because I wasn't exactly sure what to look for. I mean, it's not like there's a chapter titled: <u>WHAT TO DO WHEN YOUR ENTIRE LIFE HAS GONE TO HELL AND IT'S OBVIOUSLY ALL YOUR FAULT.</u>

Though maybe there should be.

It's like, when my parents first decided to send me here they tried to convince me that it was <u>MOSTLY</u> so I could experience life in a foreign country and enjoy a relaxing summer, and only <u>PARTLY</u> so they could shield me from what is turning out to be the world's ugliest legal grudge match.

And while I obviously did not for one second believe the <u>MOSTLY</u> part of their story, and knew it was actually more about the <u>PARTLY</u> part, the weird thing is, that for a place that's supposed to be so simple and laid-back and relaxing, how is it possible that my life has become way more complicated here than it ever was before?

For example:

1) If I thought I was stressed about holding on to my position as Amanda's good friend when I was back home, well, that's nothing compared to how freaked I am now. Because, not only has she not read my blog after that first time (which I now recognize as either an accident or fluke or an accidental fluke), but the few times she's even bothered to respond to my e-mails, she's attached photos that, to be honest, kind of hurt my feelings. Like the one of Levi and Penelope at that party. I so did <u>NOT</u> need to see that! I mean, granted, I haven't exactly confided in her about what happened between me and Levi (mostly because I know

better than to trust her), <u>BUT STILL,</u> it's just common courtesy, heck, it's common sense! And then when she sent me that pic of her and Jenna and Penelope all loaded down with Bloomingdale's bags at Fashion Island, all of them happily indulging in all of the summer fun and frolic I'm totally missing—I mean, that was completely rude and inconsiderate. Not to mention that the last I heard she was no longer even talking to Jenna. Just like I was no longer talking to Nat. It's like we'd both traded them in so we could hang with each other. That was our deal. But from the looks of their little Saturday excursion, they're now just one big happy family again, and I'm the orphan who got left in the cold. Not to mention how I can't believe she's back with Jenna after all of the <u>TRULY AWFUL</u> things she told me about her. And I cannot believe she's hanging with Jenna's cousin, Penelope (a.k.a. Levi's summer fling). Not to mention how if she can take the time to do all of those things then she can also take a few minutes out of her precious day to send me an e-mail and tell me once and for all just what the <u>HECK</u> is going on with Levi and his supposed cruise. And why he hasn't both-ered to e-mail me. And just what, if anything, he's said about me. Because I'm really starting to go into meltdown mode. But has she bothered to do any of those things? Um, that would be <u>NO!</u>

2) When I first found out that I was coming here, my worst fear was that my parents might try to kill each other while I was gone. Seriously, they were fighting so bad and so often it actually seemed like they were well on their way to dividing the house right down the center and barbequing the family pets (luckily we don't have any family pets). But still, it was really starting to mimic this old movie I once saw where the couple ended up doing exactly that, only to end up all tangled up and dead on top of their chandelier (I forget how they wound up on the chandelier, but then again that's not really the point). The point is, that now, even though none of that happened, it's somehow managed to get even worse! Because apparently my dad just got a new bachelor pad and a new girlfriend to go with it. And my mom is acting so insanely jealous that she's started calling me and confiding in me and telling me all kinds of creepy things I never wanted to know about my dad. Like she thinks she's my friend instead of my mom. And even though it's true that I'm currently experiencing a shortage of friends, it's not exactly a crisis, and I'm not exactly looking to her to fill the void.

3)  And then there's the little matter of the FOR SALE sign, which my supposed good friend Amanda just couldn't be bothered to remove, but that my former friend Natalie handled right away. And all that does is make me feel that much worse for how our friendship ended, and how she accused me of dumping her and treating her like crap. Which is not even fair since it's not like it's ENTIRELY my fault in the first place. I mean, we were both growing apart and wanted different things anyway, which, when you stop and think about it, is really neither one of our faults, because people change and grow and move on and things like that just happen. It's just the way life is. (Okay, I just reread that last part and now I feel totally creeped out since it's pretty much the exact same speech my dad gave me about the divorce.) Anyway, all of these things just lead to the next item on my list:

4)  Most of the time I feel like I don't even know who I am anymore. I'm not kidding. I feel like I'm just wandering around, trying to hang on to a home I'll probably never see again, hang on to a dad who's more interested in his new life than his old one, hang on to a friend who was probably never much of a friend to begin with, and hang on to a guy who probably doesn't even remember my name, much less the fact that he spent almost four hours kissing me and

trying to take off my dress, before using our last minute and a half together to take my virginity. And no, I really don't think he's ANONYMOUS anymore, because that kind of thinking is not only completely delusional and stark-raving mad, but also requires a certain amount of <u>OPTIMISM</u> and <u>HOPE</u> that I just can't muster. And to be honest, I haven't the slightest idea who ANONYMOUS is. But with the way things are going, I'm sure it'll turn out to be some creepy online stalker, someone who's wanted in all fifty states, including the northern and southern territories.

5) Oh yeah, and to top it all off, it's not like I've made much of an impact here. Because I really would've thought that Yannis would've stopped by and/or called by now, but, big surprise, he hasn't.

### <u>UPDATE!</u>

Believe it or not, it just went from worse to <u>EVEN WORSE!</u>

Apparently, I've now become so pathetic that even my own rescued kitty doesn't want to be with me. Seriously, just as I finished writing the above, Holly took one look at me, sniffed my shorts and T-shirt, jumped right off my bed, and scrammed out of my room as fast as he could.

Like he has a sixth sense or something.

Like he <u>KNOWS</u> what I am, and doesn't want to be beholden to a loser.

Obviously, this is probably a good time to stop writing for the night.

## CIRCLE IN THE SAND

**Blog Comments:**

**Anonymous said:**

I'm confused. From your pictures it looks like you are in paradise.

Sun, sand, sea, and a kitten . . . What more do you need?

Please explain at your earliest convenience.

**ColbyCat said:**

I don't really know how to explain, because the truth is, you're right, it is really pretty here. The beaches are nice (except for the rocky ones) and my kitten is adorable (as you can see). I guess, it's a little more barren and rugged than I usually like, but hey, you can't have everything, right?

Maybe it's just that paradise is more a state of mind than an actual place?

**Anonymous said:**

Interesting . . . I never thought of it like that.

Thanks for explaining.

July 18
To: AmandaStar
From: ColbyCat
Re: !!!!!!!!

OMG—R U serious? Levi's actually really coming here & U gave him my e-mail???

U-R-The-BEST!

!!!!!!!!!!!

Thank U Thank U Thank U!

(U sure this is 4 real & UR not messing w/me, right?)

Colby


July 18
To: NatalieZee
From: ColbyCat
Re: You're moving?
Hey Nat,

Sorry, but I really can't explain why there was an open house at my home yesterday. Though I do thank you for taking the opportunity to put all the books and CDs you borrowed back on my shelves.

And to answer your question, yes, I'm having a total blast here. And just in case you're bored, or curious, or even if you just want to know all the juicy details, you can read all about it in my blog. It's called "Circle in the Sand." And NO, I didn't name it that because of you or your mom or any of those songs she always used to sing. I just needed a summer blog name and it's the only thing I could think of on such short notice.

Well, actually, it's the second name, but whatever, just check it out if you want.

K—L8R (sorry, I know how you hate that, but I couldn't resist!)

Colby

P.S. Levi will be here soon!!!!! I can't wait!


*July 18*

*Dear Mom,*

*For your information I know all about the <u>OPEN HOUSE</u>, which means we seriously need to talk, because <u>NO WAY</u> am I moving.*

*I thought we'd been through this already?*

*This cannot continue.*

*You must stop.*

*Please contact me at your earliest convenience.*

*Love,*

*Colby*


*July 18*

*Dear Dad,*

*Mom had an <u>OPEN HOUSE</u> and I'm holding you responsible.*

*You have to do something to stop her because <u>NO WAY</u> am I moving!*

*I thought we'd been through this already?*

*This cannot continue.*

*This must stop.*

*Please contact me at your earliest convenience.*
*Love,*
*Colby*

### COLBY'S JOURNAL FOR DESPERATE TIMES
### THAT REQUIRE DESPERATE MEASURES

July 20

I don't know what's wrong with me. Seriously, you'd think I'd be happy, partly because—<u>LEVI'S COMING.</u> That's according to Amanda, who's still hooked up with Casey who happens to be best friends with Levi who said something about not being able to go to someone's surprise party because he's going on a Mediterranean cruise instead.

And also, <u>YANNIS IS COMING.</u> Here. Tonight. For a BBQ. But those two friends of his, Maria (black hair) and Christina (orange hair), who just happen to be related to one of Tassos's best friends (Christina is his friend's daughter, Maria is her cousin), are NOT invited (I made sure of that). Anyway, apparently the only reason he didn't call or come by sooner is because he had to go to Athens for a few days, and <u>NOT</u> because he suddenly decided he didn't like me, or anything remotely like that.

Please note the lack of exclamation points even though I really am excited about both of these things.

Though I must admit, the neutral punctuation is probably due to the fact that all of my excitement is currently being overshadowed by my mom and dad's last phone call, where they both informed me, under no uncertain terms, that they retain the right to divorce, date, throw open houses, and basically make a string of not just bad, but extremely reckless decisions that will surely result in the complete unraveling of my life, and quite possibly my future.

Also, I was reminded, that as a minor, there's absolutely nothing I can do about any of this, since they are the <u>ADULTS,</u> while I am merely their <u>CHILD.</u> At which point they went on to assure me that I shouldn't take everything so <u>PERSONALLY</u> as none of it is meant that way.

They are simply dedicating themselves to doing "What is in the best interest of everyone."

And all I can say to <u>THAT,</u> is:

If that's so true, and they're so <u>DEDICATED,</u> then how come they've yet to stop and consider what might be in the best interest of <u>ME</u>?

How come they can't just grow up, stay put, and:

<u>JUST LET ME GET THROUGH MY LAST YEAR OF HIGH SCHOOL MORE OR LESS UNSCATHED?</u>

Seriously.

I mean, just one more year, that's all I ask. And after that, after I graduate high school and head off to college, they're free to self-destruct or do whatever the heck they want.

Just let me complete my childhood first.

I wonder if I can divorce them?

### Colby's Journal for Desperate Times When She's So Happy She Can Hardly Breathe!

July 27

Haven't been blogging. Haven't been e-mailing. Haven't been letter writing or postcard sending. Haven't been to the Internet café. Haven't even turned on my computer in what seems like forever but is probably just over a week. And all of this is happening because:

<u>I'M CURRENTLY IMMERSED IN A VERY SERIOUS CASE OF WHAT APPEARS TO BE—MUTUAL LIKE!</u>

Ever since the night of the BBQ, when Yannis rode up on his bike and smiled at me, my stomach started doing a series of somersaults and backflips, which, to be honest, haven't really slowed down since.

But it's not the same kind of nervous and anxious feeling I had with Levi. It's more like a tingly, <u>CAN'T BELIEVE THIS IS ACTUALLY HAPPENING TO ME</u> kind of feeling. And even though I kind of felt like that back when Levi first kissed me, for some reason it's even better with Yannis.

I guess because being with Yannis feels more real, less borrowed.

Anyway, he pretty much just parked his bike, sat down beside me, and didn't really go anywhere else for the rest of the night. And the whole time we were talking and laughing and getting to know each other better, it felt like only half my brain was actually focused on what we were saying and doing, because the other half couldn't stop thinking: *I wish he'd stop talking and kiss me!*

But since Tally, Tassos, and all of their friends really weren't allowing for much in the way of privacy, I pretty much resigned myself to yet another fun, yet passion-free night.

But then, after we ate and it started to get dark, Yannis leaned toward me and whispered, "Wanna go for a ride?"

And of course I said yes.

And even though I was fully expecting to end up at that club again, this time, after riding around for a while, we ended up at his favorite beach instead. Then we parked on the road, and ran down to the sand, where he laid out a towel for us to sit on as we gazed at the moon and the stars, trying to spot the different constellations, until he finally worked up the nerve to kiss me.

That's right—<u>HE</u> had to work up the nerve to kiss <u>ME</u>!

Which means, I was making him feel just as nervous and giddy as he makes me!

Which is also the exact opposite of Levi, who pretty much assumes that every girl in any given room is totally willing to make out with him on a moment's notice. (Though to be fair, that's probably only because it's so true.)

But even though it's probably true for Yannis too, he just doesn't have that same kind of ~~confidence~~ arrogance as Levi. He's just way more polite, more respectful, and would never try to push someone to do stuff they may not be ready for.

Anyway, one minute we were talking about the Big and Little Dippers, and the next thing I knew he was kissing me. And let me just say that it was <u>TOTALLY AMAZING!</u>

Not awkward at all. Not even in the very beginning of the kiss, which is normally a pretty tense moment since both parties are striving to choreograph a duet that neither of them has ever rehearsed (at least not together).

But with Yannis, it was like both our lips just knew <u>EXACTLY</u> what to do and <u>EXACTLY</u> where to go, and it felt like magic.

In fact, it was so amazing and magical that we stayed there for hours, just kissing and talking, but mostly just kissing. Until it eventually got too cold for the shorts and T-shirts we were both wearing and he decided to take me home.

And this time when he dropped me off, he kissed me again, and said, "See you tomorrow?"

To which I just nodded and smiled and ran inside the house, thinking I would write it all down in this journal.

But in the end I chose to just lie on my bed, close my eyes, and relive it over and over again in my head, until I eventually fell asleep, where I dreamt about him too!

And sure enough, the very next day he came by again. And he's pretty much been coming by every day since!

So after just skimming through all of my previous journal entries I can hardly believe what a big whiny baby I've been. And it's so embarrassing to read all of that, I'm thinking about ripping out all of those pages and burning them at Tally and Tassos's next BBQ.

I mean, what could I possibly have been thinking? This place is <u>BEAUTIFUL</u>! It really is like <u>PARADISE,</u> only I was too blind to see it.

Granted, it may not be all that exciting or hip and trendy and jet-set and glittery like Mykonos, but when you're in the right company you really don't need all that flash.

It's like I wrote in my blog—Paradise is a state of mind!

And Yannis is just so incredibly sweet and cute and awesome, and he's even teaching me Greek! These are some of the words I've learned so far:

*Koukla Mou*—(Obviously I'm not using the Greek alphabet since our lessons haven't quite progressed that far.) Which literally means something like "my darling." Which actually sounds kind of old fashioned and weird, which is also why it's better to avoid the temptation to directly translate everything, and just take the overall gist of the word or phrase instead. Which in this case would make it more like: *honey,* or maybe even, *babe.* (Okay, still kind of weird, but I know for a fact that he means it in the nicest way!)

*Omorphos*—means pretty! (He said this about my hair on a day when I really didn't think it was looking all that *omorphos!*)

*Apothe*—means tonight! (As in, we go out just about every *apothe!* Which also happens to be true!)

*Efcharisto*—means thank you. But when I could barely get the hang of pronouncing it, Yannis told me to think of it as a person named F. Harry Stowe. Which I have to admit is so much easier!

And *Yannis*—means John. (But I still call him Yannis because it sounds way more exotic.)

Though *Colby* doesn't mean anything, it's just plain Colby. Which is what he calls me when he's not calling me *Koukla Mou.*

And, oh yah, *S'agapo* means I love you. Not that he said it or anything. Though I did ask Tassos how to say it just in case Yannis does decide to say it, then I'll know what it means. But I really hope he doesn't decide to say it because that'll just wreck everything. I mean, it's way better to keep things casual and not get all serious and over involved—just try to stay focused on having fun, and not make a bunch of false declarations and promises we'll never be able to keep.

Anyway, we actually see each other so often we've worked out a little schedule. Like, in the mornings he almost always goes to work, helping with the construction of the hotel his family is building, but in the afternoons he usually meets me and Tally and Tassos at the beach for siesta, or sometimes we just go on our own, and he always thinks it's so funny how I refuse to take off my top. But since I've yet to take it off when we're alone, I'm certainly not going to do it for the first time in front of a whole crowd of people. I mean, I actually managed to lose my virginity without once taking off my top, so why start now?

Anyway, at night we usually go into town and hang at

that club he first took me to, or we ride around on his Vespa, looking for some quiet place where we can be alone and make out.

And I have to admit that even though it's fun to hang out with all of his friends and cousins and stuff, my favorite times are always when it's just the two of us, all alone, gazing at the stars, kissing, or sometimes even just talking. And it's weird how I feel so relaxed around him, since I'm usually pretty nervous around guys (especially really cute ones like Yannis!) since it's not like I've had lots of experience with boyfriends or anything. But with Yannis, everything feels so natural and easy and comfortable.

Which, again, is pretty much the exact opposite of how I felt with Levi.

Though of course, wouldn't you know it, just as I'd given up, just as I decided to move on and forget about him completely, Levi decides to e-mail me about his upcoming cruise, and now I don't know what I'm supposed to do. I mean, luckily he's not coming HERE, because that would be really awkward now that I'm hanging out with Yannis so much. But still, he is going to MYKONOS, which is just a short boat ride away.

If I choose to make the journey, that is.

I mean, I've been DYING to go to Mykonos this whole entire time, or at least since my plane landed there and the guy I sat next to told me it was the only island worth visiting. Only now that I have an actual excuse to get on the ferry and go, I'm no longer sure that I want to.

Though luckily I have a little over a week to decide.

Okay, I can hear Yannis's bike in the drive, but let me write one more thing that's kind of been bothering me in the midst of all this incredible happiness:

I'm not sure why, but I haven't exactly been truthful with him about my life back home. I mean, I guess it's because it's just such a relief to be hanging out and having fun and not thinking about any of my problems that it kind of makes me reluctant to bring it up.

Though if I'm really going to be honest, then I also have to admit that the other reason is that I don't want him to think of me as sad, or pathetic, or worse. Because even though I've only met his cousins and his little brother, Christos, and I haven't met his parents or anything, when he talks about them, he always says such nice things that it makes me feel kind of weird to talk about mine. Especially since I'm not thinking so well of them at the moment. I mean, truth be told, I'm so upset, angry, and disgusted with them, I don't even think I could fake it if I tried. And I just can't bear to have Yannis think I'm a loser, or that my home life is one big disaster.

Even though it is.

Because right now he sees me as this happy-go-lucky, free-spirited, California girl. (Okay, one who won't take her top off, but still.) And that's the way I'm determined to keep it.

Okay, he's knocking on my bedroom door—so—gotta run!

COLBY'S JOURNAL FOR DESPERATE TIMES WHEN SHE'S
DESPERATELY, DELIRIOUSLY, SERIOUSLY LIKING SOMEONE

August 1

So last night Yannis took me to dinner. And even though it wasn't exactly the first time we'd eaten a meal together, it was the first time we'd eaten a meal without being chaperoned by Tally, Tassos, his little brother, or any one of his hundreds of cousins and friends. We even went to a restaurant that was a non-cousin-owned establishment. And I know, because I checked.

Anyway, it was awesome.

And dreamy.

And magical!

But all that magic actually started when he came to the house to get me, and I opened the door and felt my heart skip a beat—seriously! I mean, even though we see each other every single day, something about seeing him standing in the doorway, all dressed up, with flowers in hand (Yes! He even brought me flowers!), smiling like he really was happy to see me, well, it made it seem like the very first time all over again.

Maybe it was the cool jeans he was wearing, or the nicely pressed shirt, or the way his deep green eyes gazed into mine. Maybe it was the way he smiled, so genuine and warm and inviting. Or maybe it was the way his arm felt so right when he slipped it around my waist.

Whatever it was, I felt like pinching myself, since I

could hardly believe that this wonderful, cute, sweet, amazing guy had shown up just for me!

Anyway, when we got to the restaurant, they led us to a table in this tiny but beautiful courtyard that was all lit up by candles and moonlight. There was music playing in the background, and everything about it was just so perfect and romantic and amazing—the kind of night you always dream about, or see in movies, but doubt you'll ever experience for yourself.

So after this great dinner that included all kinds of food I can't pronounce, much less spell, we walked around town for a while before stopping by our favorite club to say hi to some friends and hang for a little while, before getting back on the bike and heading over to our favorite beach.

And I don't know if it was the caffeine (I had two and a half Cokes at dinner), or the moon (it was round and full and amazingly bright), or just that wonderful, expansive feeling of being so far from home and so free, but before I could even stop to think about what I was doing, I stripped off my dress and ran straight into the sea.

So of course, Yannis stripped off his shirt and pants and followed.

And then we swam, and splashed, and chased each other through the surf, going under, popping back up, until he eventually caught up with me. And when he turned me to face him, he kissed me in a way that reminded me of that very first night—back when we were new and hesitant and full of wonder.

And when I opened my eyes I saw his green ones gazing into mine, and his dark, wet curls curving against the sides of his face, and the clusters of water droplets shining silver in the moonlight as they clung to his tan, bare skin.

And he was so beautiful, and so tempting, and so alluring, and so immediately <u>THERE,</u> that I yanked free of his arms and ran right back to shore, struggling to get back in my dress before something happened to change my mind—unwilling to make the same mistake twice.

Then we lay on the sand and held hands, both of us enveloped in silence and darkness, as I closed my eyes and tried to capture the moment, willing it to never end.

August 3
To: Levi501
From: ColbyCat
Re: UR cruise
Hey Levi,

I jus got UR msg & 2 answer UR ? I'm not in Mykonos, I'm in Tinos. Tho I can C Mykonos bcuz it's pretty close by. So I'll def try 2 meet up w/U. Jus lemme no the xact day & time, K?

Ciao—
Colby

## CIRCLE IN THE SAND

**Blog Comments:**

**Anonymous said:**

Where are you?

Please don't tell me you've given up on your blog?

**ColbyCat said:**

I'm back, it was merely a brief vacation, I assure you!

## CIRCLE IN THE SAND

August 3

I'm back! And no, <u>ANONYMOUS,</u> I have not given up on my blog. Though I have discovered a little something I like to call <u>GETTING A LIFE.</u> And now that I've got one, I find it's taking up most of my time. Though apparently you're not the only one who missed me, because Petros actually gave me <u>A HUG</u> when I walked through the door! He said he was sure I'd gone back to America without even saying good-bye (which I would never, ever do!). But even though he claimed to be relieved and happy to see me, he still made me pay for my frappe. (Though according to his son, Stavros, the fact that I even got one free drink out of him is a bona fide miracle!)

So without further delay, here are some pictures for you to enjoy—

1) That is a picture of me attempting to windsurf. Can you believe it? My friend Yannis is actually really good at it, and he was determined to teach me, so I could be good at it too. But please don't be too impressed by what you see here, because the truth is, that photo was taken during the two and a half seconds I actually managed to stay up! Because, trust me, just one second later, I fell ack-basswards into the water!

2) That is a picture of Mr. Holly Golightly—notice how much bigger (and cuter!) he's gotten! Though he still gets all pissy whenever I try to cuddle him too much.

3) That is a picture of Tassos's studio, where he makes the most beautiful marble sculptures (Tinos has a very famous marble sculpting school where Tassos sometimes teaches) and pottery and stuff, don't you agree? Though don't be fooled by the simplicity of it, because it is way, WAY harder than it looks. Seriously. When he sat me down at the potter's wheel and tried to teach me how to do it, I failed. BIG-TIME. And what was supposed to be my vase totally collapsed and became nothing more than a big, runny lump of clay.

4) See that big, runny lump of clay? That's my vase. I so wasn't kidding.

5) That's a picture of Yannis petting Holly. Notice how he has no scratches on his arms. I have a terrible suspicion that Holly actually likes him better than me even though I'm the one who saved him from starvation. Apparently cats have short memories. Which means my next pet will be an elephant.

6) That's me and Yannis at the club, just hanging with some friends. See that guy standing behind me? That's Yannis's cousin. And the guy standing next to him? Also his cousin. And the girl in the far right corner? Yup, you guessed it, another cousin. And that guy next to me? That's his little brother, Christos. Ha! You thought it was another cousin, didn't you?

7) That's me and Yannis at the beach. Notice how it appears to be just us? But don't be fooled, one of his cousins was actually taking the picture.

8) Me and Yannis at one of Tally and Tassos's Saturday BBQs, where he's teaching me the actual steps to that Greek dance I thought I knew, because contrary to what I originally thought, you're not really supposed to just run in a circle, there are very specific steps, and it's much more intricate than I ever would've/could've imagined.

9) That's me and Yannis drinking frappes with some of his cousins at an outdoor café on the harbor. Frappe rocks. It's seriously growing on me. Especially that free one that Petros gave me that one time. That was definitely the best one yet!

Okay, that's it!

Hope this makes up for my little break—
ANONYMOUS!

Love,

Colby


August 4

To: NatalieZee

From: ColbyCat

Re: Who's Yannis?

Hey Nat,

Yannis is a friend of mine.

A really good friend.

Actually, I guess he's kind of like my boyfriend. Though it's not like you need to tell anyone that or spread it around town, okay?

I mean, not that I think you would or anything, but still, I just feel like I should say it, since it could be kind of weird if word got out since Levi will be coming here soon.

Though maybe that still makes it more weird HERE than THERE?

See, I really haven't changed as much as you think. I'm still just as crazy and confused as ever!

Okay, well, thanks for reading my blog!

Hope your summer is going well—

Colby

August 4
To: AmandaStar
From: ColbyCat
Re: UR blog/Sandal Guy
Hey Amanda,

Thx 4 ckg out my blog. But no, Yannis is so NOT my boyfriend. He's just a friend. U no, someone 2 hang w/ every now & then so I don't die of xtreme boredom over here.

And 2 answer UR ? yes, believe it or not, most of the guyz around here wear sandals like that. But I guess IV just been stuck here 4 so long now I'm starting 2 get used 2 it. I mean, I hardly even notice them NEmore. At least not until U mentioned it.

Which is really pretty scary if U think about it!

So Levi will be in Mykonos in just 3 days, & I sooo can't wait!

I'll let you know how it goes ☺
K—C—YA—
Colby


## CIRCLE IN THE SAND

**Blog Comments:**

**Anonymous said:**

Who is Yannis?

**ColbyCat said:**

A friend.

**Anonymous said:**

Tell me more about this friend.

**ColbyCat said:**

What do you want to know?

**Anonymous said:**

Is he your boyfriend?

**ColbyCat said:**

Define boyfriend.

**Anonymous said:**

The opposite of boy friend.

**ColbyCat said:**

Define boy friend.

**Anonymous said:**

You like to play games.

**ColbyCat said:**

You're the one who goes by ANONYMOUS!

**Anonymous said:**

True.

**ColbyCat said:**

Have you ever considered not being ANONYMOUS anymore?

**Anonymous said:**

Yes. I have considered it.

**ColbyCat said:**

And???

**Anonymous said:**

And I am still considering it.

**ColbyCat said:**

Okay, let me know what you decide.

COLBY'S JOURNAL FOR DESPERATE TIMES WHEN
SHE'S GOTTEN HERSELF INTO SUCH A MESS
SHE CAN'T FIND HER WAY OUT

August 7

Leave it to me to take a monumentally great thing and mess it up in such a hugely colossal way that there's just no fixing it. I mean, just when I was starting to be really happy, just when I was starting to think that my life was so great it was almost too good to be true—WHAM! I make sure that it isn't.

I mean, let's face it, I can barely handle one guy, much less two, so none of this should come as any kind of surprise to anyone, especially me. I guess I've just never been the kind of girl who can string 'em along and leave 'em begging for more, like Amanda, and practically everyone else in my cool new group (well, maybe I should've written FORMER cool new group instead, since, at the moment, I'm not exactly part of it anymore, and they haven't exactly given me any indication of missing me, much less remembering me).

Anyway, I guess I'm just too serious, too dorky, too nervous, too big of a geek, too honest—except when I lie. Because every time I try to lie about something, the lie somehow manages to get so out of control, expanding and growing so big it practically takes on a life of its own, a life that eventually sets out to destroy my very own.

I guess that's what Tally and Tassos refer to as *karma*. Getting what you give.

So anyway, last night, when Yannis picked me up, he was acting all cute and sly and mysterious about where we were going. And even though I kept trying to guess, he just kept shaking his head, saying, "You'll see."

So when we finally ended up at what basically seemed to be a big construction site, I climbed off the back of his Vespa, took one look around and said, "Okay, I give up."

But he just laughed, grabbed my hand, and tried to lead me inside. And when I hesitated by the front door, he kissed me on the cheek and said, "Relax, it belongs to my family, I just want to show you around." Then he proceeded to give me a tour of the hotel he's been working on all summer, but that probably won't be completely finished until sometime this winter. And by the way he was smiling and pointing out all the little details, all of the things that were either his idea or that he'd personally worked on or built by himself, it was obvious he was really excited about showing it to me.

But no matter how proud he was, no matter how anxious he was for me to share in his excitement, I just couldn't match it.

I was too busy staring at his sandals.

Yup, the same exact sandals that I never even noticed until Amanda made that nasty comment about them in her e-mail.

But now that she had, all I could do was gaze at his feet and think—*What the heck are you doing, Colby?*

And even though I knew I was being <u>SHALLOW. SOOO INCREDIBLY SHALLOW.</u>

I just couldn't help it.

Though I wish that were all, I wish I could say it stopped there, because unfortunately, it gets worse.

Because suddenly, the very same accent that, just yesterday, I found so adorable and sexy, started to grate on my nerves. And I found myself cringing every time he uttered something from his version of the cool American phrase book.

Stuff like:

*Relax, it's no problem.*

Or: *Slow down, it's no worries.*

Even his own language started to bug me, like when he, for the one millionth time, referred to me as: *Koukla Mou.*

It's like, practically overnight, with just one stupid, bitchy e-mail from Amanda, I started questioning everything about him, about <u>US!</u> Like I'd completely lost the ability to see anything as I once had. Like I literally went from thinking I might really, really, really like him, to not even responding when he told me he loved me.

That's right, he told me he loved me.

After we'd concluded the tour of the lobby, the reception, the kitchen, the bar, the gym, and a few of the other rooms and suites, he led me out to the pool area, that he just happened to have all set up with chairs and blankets and candles and music and food and drinks and flowers. And it should've been really romantic, because it <u>WAS</u> really romantic, except for the fact that the whole entire time all I could do was continue to stare at his shoes, cringe at his accent, and think:

*What the heck are you doing, Colby? Summer will soon be over. August 31 is just around the corner. Levi will be here tomorrow. And now you have to make a choice.*

You can either:

1) Stop being so shallow, and allow yourself to fall for this guy who up until yesterday you thought you really, really liked, and who happens to be really cute, nice, sweet, kind, and fun, and who, through no real fault of his own, just happens to overuse some weird phrases, in a weird accent, that you've just now decided gets on your nerves, and yes, who also happens to wear sandals that are so bizarre you can barely stand to look at his feet, even though you can't seem to stop staring at them. **OR:**

2) You can focus on your future, and get the heck out of here! Because even though Amanda is undisputedly shallow, to the point where it just might be contagious, the fact that she even bothered to write you back and read your blog in the first place proves you're still <u>IN.</u> Not to mention how Levi is coming all this way to see you. Or at least he plans to see you because he's coming all this way. At any rate, if you have half a brain left in your cloudy, foggy, overcast head, you will choose Levi and Amanda and prom and parties, which is the only <u>SOCIAL SECURITY</u> plan you currently have. <u>BECAUSE GREECE IS NOT YOUR FUTURE, BUT CALIFORNIA IS!</u>

3) Not to mention how <u>YOU</u> of all people should be very well versed in how <u>LOVE NEVER LASTS!</u> It's just another illusion that people like to fool themselves into believing. And even if, by some small chance, it did turn out to be valid, real, and mutual, it's still just a matter of time before it ends anyway, so really, what's the point of even going there? Just look at your parents, if you need further proof. Or half of Hollywood! Love is invisible, unreal! Besides, everything has a beginning, middle, and end and you're a complete sappy fool if you allow yourself to believe otherwise!

But what I also haven't mentioned until now, is that earlier in the day, when I was getting ready to leave the café, I saw Yannis standing by the harbor, right there in the fish market, talking to Maria. And even though they weren't doing anything other than just talking, seeing them together like that still managed to make my stomach go all queasy and weird, almost like someone had kicked it—really, really hard, right in the center of my gut.

And just after I thought: *Why is he in town, talking to Maria, when just last night he said he'd be working all day?*

I thought: *Why does it even matter? YOU don't live here. And this is nothing more than a fun, summer fling to keep you from dying of boredom! Soon you'll be going home and you'll never even see him again. And if Yannis wants to be with Maria—what's it to you? You just need to focus on yourself and get your priorities straight! You've had your fun, and now it's time to make a quick exit, get the heck out before you start believing you feel stuff that's not even real!*

But still, even though I knew all that to be true, it's not like it stopped the horrible pang in my gut, my shortness of breath, or the hectic beating of my heart, as I watched Maria lean in and kiss Yannis, once on each cheek.

So after Yannis lit all the candles and turned on the music, he pulled me into his arms, brushed his lips against my hair, and whispered, *"S'agapo,"* so softly I almost didn't hear it.

Except that I did hear it.

I just pretended I didn't.

And instead of responding, I just grabbed us each a Coke and started pouring them into some glasses. And for the rest of the night I just went through the motions, playing the part of a girl who was enjoying a fun, romantic, lighthearted date.

But all the while, deep down inside, I was thinking about which ferry I should catch ~~tomorrow~~ (now technically today), which would get me to Mykonos in time to see Levi.

And even though it may sound horrible, shallow, stupid, and disgusting.

In the end, I was only trying to be practical.

Because the fact is, Yannis doesn't go to Harbor High, but Levi does.

And I never should've let things go this far to begin with.

August 7
To: Levi501
From: ColbyCat
Re: Mykonos!
Hey Levi,

I'm going to catch the 1:00 ferry, so I'll meet U @ the dock when you get in.

C U soon—

Colby

# CIRCLE IN THE SAND

August 7

Just stopping in for a quick hello because in just a few hours I'll be headed <u>HERE</u>!

Yup, that's a picture of <u>MYKONOS!!!</u>

And I can hardly wait to see it for myself, since I've been dying to go there this whole, entire time!

Anyway, a very good friend of mine from home is visiting there, so I'm planning to hop on the ferry and go visit. So hopefully I will have lots of photos to share with you tomorrow! (Or the next day—since I'm really not sure when I'll be getting back!)

So—

*Kalo Takseethee* to me!

(That's phonetic Greek for *Bon Voyage!*)

Colby

# CIRCLE IN THE SAND

**Blog Comments:**

**Anonymous said:**

What's in Mykonos?

**ColbyCat said:**

Windmills, so they tell me.

**Anonymous said:**

What else?

**ColbyCat said:**

A world-famous pelican!

**Anonymous said:**

And?

**ColbyCat said:**

Wild nightlife?

**Anonymous said:**

Which are you most looking forward to? The windmills, the world-famous pelican, or the wild nightlife?

**ColbyCat said:**

Is this a test?

**Anonymous said:**

No, just a question.

**ColbyCat said:**

Then I'll tell you when I get back. Though mostly I'm going to visit my friend.

**Anonymous said:**

Which friend?

**ColbyCat said:**

Tell me who you are and I'll tell you who he is. Deal?

**Anonymous said:**

No deal.

**ColbyCat said:**

Your choice.

*August 7*
*Dear Aunt Tally and Tassos,*

I'm leaving this note on the fridge since you always head straight for it when you get back from the beach, so I figured you'd find it right away.

Anyway, I probably should have told you this before, but I'm taking the ferry to Mykonos. Though <u>PLEASE</u> don't rush down to the dock to come get me, because, the truth is, by the time you read this, I'll be gone.

Also, please don't worry, or stress, or anything like that because I'll be totally fine, and it's not like I'm mad at you, or trying to run away from home, or anything remotely like that. I just—well, let's just say that I'm meeting up with A Friend. Someone I know from school. And I'll probably be back late tonight, or maybe even tomorrow morning, since I forgot to find out how long my friend is staying. But if my friend stays overnight then I probably will too. Just to keep my friend company, since I don't know if my friend is traveling with other friends.

Okay, so I guess I'll see you either tonight or tomorrow, but please, don't come to Mykonos and try to look for me or anything, because:

1) I'll be totally fine. &
2) That would be totally embarrassing.

Okay, well, thanks for understanding. (I really hope you understand, but if not I'll explain it all to you when I get back either tonight or tomorrow, I promise.)

Love,

Colby

P.S. If Yannis comes over can you please just tell him that I'm sick, or not feeling well, or something like that? And if he still insists on trying to see me then can you please just inform him that I'm so sick and unwell that I'm not up to seeing anyone but that I will see him tomorrow, for sure?

P.P.S. Sorry about asking you to lie, because I know you think it's bad karma. But trust me, it's going toward a very good cause, which I will also explain later.

*August 7*
*Dear Mom,*

This postcard is not lying because the fact is, I really am in Mykonos. And from what I've seen so far, this is where you and Dad should've sent me in the first place. Because not only is it beautiful, but it's also cool and fun and way more exciting than Tinos. I mean, nothing against Aunt Tally, because she's really nice and <u>NOT AT ALL CRAZY</u> like you guys always said, and it's not like it's her fault that Tinos is totally boring compared to Mykonos.

*And even though you're probably wondering why I'm here, I'm not going to tell you. I mean, it's not like you've been all that honest either, since I happen to know all about your new boyfriend even though you think that I don't. Though I guess we'll save that for an actual letter where there's more room to write.*

*Love,*
*Your disillusioned daughter,*
*Colby*

*August 7*
*Dear Dad,*

*The front of this postcard features a picture of some very famous windmills that are located in Mykonos, which is where I am now. Though I won't tell you why since even though you managed to tell me about Mom's new boyfriend, you failed to mention the fact of how you are now living with your girlfriend. Though I guess we'll just have to save that little conversation for one of those fun family conference calls you and Mom seem so fond of.*

*Thank you for curing me of my unbridled optimism.*

*Love,*
*Colby*

*August 7*
*Dear Nat,*

*I know you're probably pretty surprised to get a postcard from me, but I'm in Mykonos, sitting at the dock, waiting for Levi's boat to come in, and I'm kind of bored, and needed something to do, so I figured I'd send you a card.*

*Anyway, it's really pretty here, just like it looks in the picture, and, well, I think I see his boat so—*
*Take care,*
*Colby*

*August 7*
*Dear Amanda,*

*OMG—Levi's boat just got here, but I thought I'd say a quick HEY! since I haven't sent you any postcards since I got here. Anyway, obviously I haven't been to that beach yet—though maybe I'll go there with Levi—who knows?*
*Okay, he's here, so—*
*Later—*
*Colby*

## CIRCLE IN THE SAND

August 8

This post will be short and sweet because I'm TOTALLY EXHAUSTED! But that's probably only because I just got off the boat from Mykonos and came straight here to the café to download some of these photos, which probably wasn't the best idea since I've been up all night and I look pretty ratty, to the point where Petros is actually shaking his head and scowling at me from behind the counter. Not to mention how he refused to make me a frappe when I ordered one.

Instead he took one look at me and said, "No coffee for you! You look terrible! Like gypsy! Go home!"

Yup, you always know where you stand with Petros.

And since he seems pretty dang serious about sending me home, and is probably just seconds away from evicting me, I'll make it snappy!

1) Behold the famous Mykonian windmills. Pretty, huh?

2) The famous Mykonian pelican as seen from afar! And yes I know there are pelicans in Tinos too, but they're not exactly famous now are they?

3) The famous Mykonian wild nightlife! And just so you know, I took this picture especially for YOU, ANONYMOUS. But to be honest, out of all of these things, I have to admit that I liked #4 the best!

4) This is Little Venice, my favorite place of all! Probably because it was just so romantic, with the way the water laps right up against the buildings, just like the real Venice (even though I've never actually been, I've seen pictures). The funny thing is that this wasn't originally on my list of things to see. But my friend had a guidebook, and this place was definitely recommended. And even though this is not the best picture—I still think you can see why they'd suggest it.

5) This is a picture of Super Paradise beach, though we only stayed long enough for me to snap this

picture, because it was full of naked and/or nearly naked gay guys, which totally freaked out my friend.

6) Here's a picture of my friend and me at Paradise beach. It should be noted that this photo was graciously taken by an older, completely naked, German lady. And believe me, Levi's the one who asked her to take our picture, not me! Also notice how Levi and I are both fully clothed—trust me, we were the only ones!

7) Here is a club—I forget the name, but just know that it got even more crowded and wild than what you see in this picture. And yes, that guy dancing on top of the bar REALLY IS wearing nothing more than a black leather thong and motorcycle boots—your eyes are NOT deceiving you—though you probably wish they were!

8) Here's a picture of the motorbike that Levi crashed twice, even though he swears it wasn't his fault. The scratches are ours, though I solemnly swear that big dent on the side was already there when we got it! Scout's honor!

9) Here's a photo of me, lying on the beach, watching the sunrise.

10) Here's a photo of Levi waving good-bye as he boards his cruise ship.

11) Here's a photo of the ferry that took me back to Tinos.

12) Here's a photo of Petros scowling at me just seconds

after he told me to go home. See how his mustache is twitching to where it almost looks animated? That's how I know he's serious. Though, truth be told, he just might have a point. I am pretty sleepy so—

Later—
Colby

## CIRCLE IN THE SAND

**Blog Comments:**

**Anonymous said:**
Looks like you had a nice trip. I am also going away. Though it's been nice knowing you.

**ColbyCat said:**
Where are you going?

**Anonymous said:**
Away.

**ColbyCat said:**
Okay . . . but are you coming back?

**Anonymous said:**
Not likely.

**ColbyCat said:**

So that's it? You're just going to disappear into blog oblivion without ever revealing yourself?

**Anonymous said:**

It seems so.

**ColbyCat said:**

That doesn't seem fair.

**Anonymous said:**

That's life.

COLBY'S JOURNAL FOR DESPERATE TIMES WHEN
SHE'S MESSED UP HER LIFE SO BAD SHE HAS
NOWHERE ELSE TO GO BUT HERE

August 10

According to one of my aunt Tally's books, this is how karma works:

Action–Reaction

Reap–Sow

What goes around comes around.

What you give you get.

Though it's not like I need a book to explain it, because, believe me, right now I'm living it. And all I can think is that I must have put some seriously bad energy out there, because I'm definitely getting some serious payback now.

This is what I'm dealing with:

1) A not-so-happy, not-so-mellow, Aunt Tally and Tassos, who cannot get over the fact that I island hopped without their consent.

2) A boyfriend (?) who no longer comes over, no longer speaks to me, probably never really loved me, and I have no idea why. Though I did see him talking to Maria (again!) at the port, day before yesterday, when I'd just gotten back from Mykonos and was leaving the café, (and no, he didn't see me) so maybe I actually do know why.

3) An e-mail from Natalie telling me that the FOR SALE sign in front of my house has now been exchanged for one that says: SOLD.

4) A brief phone call from my mother who assures me she no longer wants to move to Arizona now that she's fallen for her (much younger) personal trainer, who, she informs me, is actually a <u>REAL LIVE PERSON</u> and <u>NOT</u> a cliché like I think.

5) A father who is too busy to call and/or send a note because he's apparently not just shacking up with, but is now engaged to his (also much younger, at least according to my mom) girlfriend, even though the divorce is not yet final, and may never be with the way they're battling over <u>EVERYTHING.</u>

6) An ANONYMOUS person who has gladly taken his or her place in the everexpanding line for "People Who Would Like to Register a Complaint About Just How Bad Colby Sucks," since he/she pretty much abandoned my blog in a big fat hurry with no explanation whatsoever.

7) A cat that apparently also thinks I suck since I recently discovered that when I left for Mykonos, I was in such a hurry to flee, I forgot to leave Holly's window open—and so far he's yet to return.

And all of that would be fine, had my clandestine field trip actually been worth it. But the truth is, it so wasn't. And all I've got to show for it now is:

_____(Nothing.)

Seriously, I'm just as empty as I was the day I first got here. Only now I get to return home to even less than what I started with.

So basically, Mykonos was a total bust, and this is why:

I admit, I couldn't have been more surprised when Levi got off the boat with his mom and dad and little sister and brother in tow. In fact, I was <u>SHOCKED.</u> I mean now, looking back, of course it seems pretty obvious that a seventeen-year-old guy isn't actually going to embark on a solo Mediterranean cruise. Yet for some reason, that's exactly what I'd convinced myself of. I was just so sure that Levi was traveling all this way, and only tolerating the stops in Capri and Crete, just so he could get to Mykonos and enjoy a long, leisurely, romantic evening with me.

Stupid, I know. But since that's only the first in a whole succession of stupid things I've done lately, we'll just refer to it as Stupid Exhibit #1.

Anyway, I can't say Levi's family was exactly what I expected either. Though, I guess they weren't exactly the opposite of what I expected, since I really wasn't expecting them in the first place. Nor had I given them any real thought before the moment they were standing right before me.

Though if I had, I hope I would've been generous, hopeful, and kind enough to imagine something better than how they actually were, because as it turned out, they were kind of embarrassing.

First of all, Levi's dad is <u>REALLY LOUD.</u> I mean, seriously loud. And now I know why foreigners always say Americans are loud—it's because a lot of us are. It's like somehow he got the idea that if he spoke in a really loud voice, to the point where he was practically screaming, the Greeks would better understand him. But even if that tactic did somehow manage to work, for the most part it seemed pretty unnecessary, since from what I could tell most of the Mykonians speak really good English, and don't exactly need to be yelled at.

And then his mom, well, I don't mean to be rude or

judgmental, and it's not like I think my mom's all that great at the moment either, but all she pretty much wanted to do was go on a guided tour of jewelry stores. As though the whole point to traveling abroad was so she could conduct an extensive study of minimalls, with ours always coming out on top. Seriously, when I mentioned going to Paraportiani, or the windmills, or the beaches, she'd just squint at Mr. Bonham and go, "How far away is that, Jim?"

Though I refuse to say anything bad about his little brother and sister. I mean, even though they were kind of spoiled and bratty and basically horrible, it's not like you couldn't see where they got it.

So anyway, getting back to the dock, the moment I saw them I did my best to just swallow my disappointment and shock, and not gawk at the size of his entourage. And then I waved both my arms in the air, going back and forth, forth and back, like scissor kicks, until Levi finally saw me. And after he mumbled something sounding like—*hey,* his dad marched right up and gave me this seriously firm handshake like we'd just closed a business deal, while his mom just stood there beside him, looking me up and down and squinting at me until she lowered her sunglasses and squinted some more.

Then his little brother laughed, and his little sister stared, as Levi leaned in to give me the world's most awkward supervised hug.

And then his dad lifted his arm to his forehead, and

just as I thought he was about to salute me, he made himself a little hand visor and surveyed the landscape. Then he dropped it just as quickly, and turned to me and said, "So, what are you going to show us first?"

And since I'd only been on Mykonos about twenty minutes longer than they had, I'd pretty much only seen the gift shop where I'd bought some postcards, and the dock where we were standing. So I just shrugged and did my best to explain how it was my first visit too. That I was actually living on that little island, just right over there, the one you can see if you look straight across the water, at an angle.

And after all five of them had craned their necks, they turned back to me, disappointment clearly stamped across every one of their faces, their dreams of a private Greek island tour suddenly dashed.

Then Mrs. Bonham handed Mr. Bonham the guidebook she carries in her purse, and after intense study of the section titled: WHERE TO SHOP & DINE, all five of us went clomping through town, wandering through streets so narrow and winding at times we were actually forced to walk single file. And every now and then, Mr. Bonham (our fearless leader) would look back at me and say, "Do all the buildings in Tinos look alike too? Because I can't tell one of these from the other. It all looks the same. Can't tell 'em apart!"

Or his mom would squint at me, purse her lips, and go, "Is Tinos this—*quaint* as well?" And the way she said *quaint,* it was pretty obvious that what she really meant was *small-time.*

But by the time they started asking me why the Greeks all—<u>FILL IN THE STUPID QUESTIONS BLANK,</u> I'd given up trying to entertain and inform them with my answers, and just started shrugging instead.

I mean, first of all, I'm certainly no authority on the Greeks, their islands, or why they do just about anything they do. Because the truth is, I'd spent the majority of the summer focused on one thing—trying to stay connected to home (which would be Item #2 on the Stupid Exhibit tour). And the one Greek I had allowed myself to get close to, I was currently betraying (that would be Item #3). So excuse me for being more than a little reluctant to speak on his, or his people's behalf.

So after a concentrated, quickie tour of every single gold store the town of Mykonos had to offer, after Mr. Bonham had successfully saved himself the equivalent of five U.S. dollars by bargaining down the price of an eighteen-karat gold Greek key design necklace in the loudest voice imaginable, all five Bonhams decided they were starved, and consulted the guidebook to see where they could get a hamburger.

That's right, <u>A HAMBURGER.</u> Just like the kind you can get back home, or, I don't know, maybe on their cruise ship, you know, the one that was docked in the harbor?

"Don't you want to maybe try a gyro?" I suggested. "They're really good, kind of like a Greek hamburger," I said, having grown quite fond of them in the short time I'd been in Tinos.

"Oh, I'd love to try one myself." Mrs. Bonham smiled in that tight, squinty way I'd come to know as her signature smirk. "But Salem and Duncan really prefer to keep it simple. They don't always do so well with these foreign foods," she whispered, motioning to the twelve- and thirteen-year-olds, blaming it all on them.

So, we headed to a taverna. One that was chock full of people they recognized from the boat. And while we were seated at the table, each of us hunched over our meals, chewing quietly and staring into space, I couldn't help but notice how different Levi was, how he suddenly seemed so opposite of the way he was at home, the way I'd remembered him.

I mean, at home he's like this uber-cool deity, the undisputed king who rules the school. But seeing him sitting across from me, dragging a fistful of fries through some ketchup as he admired his silver ring, I couldn't help but notice just how fake and phony and almost empty he seemed. Like he was so caught up in his clothes and his hair and his jewelry and his image, that there was no room left for anything else.

So then of course, the second after I thought that, I felt horrible, terrible, and guilty. I mean, so far, all I'd done was spend the entire afternoon judging them. Just like I'd spent all of the previous night judging Yannis. And it made me wonder if maybe I was the one who should be judged. Maybe the problem wasn't them at all.

Maybe the problem was <u>ME.</u> Maybe I was the one with no personality or identity. Maybe I was the one who was empty inside.

Because the truth is, when I gazed at all of them again, watching as they enjoyed their meal in silence, obviously feeling content with their lives and each other, I realized I was the exact opposite of content. That while these people knew exactly who they were, what they stood for, and seemed to be entirely at peace with it all, I myself was as lost and clueless as ever.

I had no idea what I was doing.

And lately, I didn't seem to stand for much of anything.

I mean, here I'd somehow convinced myself that I'd been humming along, making some major life progress, when all along I'd been slowly unraveling at the seams and was too dumb to notice.

For example—Stupid Exhibit #4 (obviously, none of these exhibits are in actual chronological order):

I'd been friends with Natalie Zippenhoffer for practically my whole entire life, and even though she's nice, and smart, and interesting, and real (and yes, a major geek), and even though we have tons of things in common (like the fact that I'm a major geek too, and we like the same books, songs, and movies—which are mostly all the books, songs, and movies that nobody even knows about, much less likes), I didn't even hesitate when it came time to throw her overboard. It's like the second I got a shot at being visible and cool via hanging with Amanda, into the water Natalie went.

I guess I just felt so flattered that someone who's as popular and important as Amanda would even want to speak to me, much less hang out with me. Not to mention how I hoped she'd be able to make me popular and important too. I just wanted to be known for something more than high test scores. So every time she wasn't so nice (which was pretty frequent), and every time she made fun of all the things I like (which was pretty much all the time), I either completely ignored it or pretended I no longer liked those things either. Then I did my frantic best to avoid Natalie when I passed her in the hall, so I could stay in good with Amanda.

So when I got my shot at Levi Bonham, I knew I hit the big time.

It was only after spending the day with his family, in a foreign place that's like a million miles away from everything that once made him so cool, that I could barely remember what the attraction was to begin with.

I mean, of course he was still gorgeous, anyone could see that, since it's not like distance and a new time zone could ever mess with his cool, movie star looks. Only now he seemed gorgeous in a way that was too intentional, too calculated, too premeditated, as though being cute had become a full-time endeavor, and something about that just really bugged me.

Anyway, after we finished our meals and his dad settled the check, his family decided they had "done" Mykonos and were eager to head back to the boat. Making it clear that Levi was free to stay and dance the night away with me.

So he did. I mean, we did. Though we didn't exactly start with dancing, since it was still early and really hot out. So I, thinking it might be fun to hit the beaches, managed to convince him to rent a Vespa together. But after we crashed it twice (not badly, but both times his fault) I insisted on taking over, since it was obvious he just couldn't get the hang of working the clutch since it's on the foot pedal, which, of course, I'd totally mastered thanks to Yannis's lesson in "Vespa Riding and Safety 101."

But even though we didn't crash again, it was pretty obvious that my sitting in front, taking charge of the driving, wasn't going over so well with him. It was like his whole alpha-male, he-man, jock persona just couldn't handle giving up control to a girl.

So when we finally made it to the beach with the very best name of them all—Super Paradise, he totally freaked when he saw it was full of mostly naked, mostly gay, guys. And I mean, <u>FREAKED.</u> Like he thought all that nudity and gayness was somehow contagious.

So then of course we had to get right back on the bike and head over to just plain old Paradise beach, which just happened to be filled with row after row of topless and/or nude girls. Which of course made him bug me about taking my top off, but only for a little while since there were plenty of other breasts for him to ogle. And believe me, did he ogle. I mean head swiveling, eye bugging, tongue hanging and dripping with drool kind of ogling. And he was so obvious about it I was actually kind of embarrassed to be sitting next to him. Because no matter how many times I've been to the beach with Yannis, I've never once seen him carry on like that. And even though that's probably because he's used to it, having grown up like that and all, I'm really not joking or exaggerating when I write that Levi was RIDICULOUS. Seriously, even after the sun went down and there were only a few people left, I practically had to drag him by the arms and legs just to get him out of there.

So then, because we were in Mykonos, and because that's what you're supposed to do when you're in Mykonos, we hit the clubs. I mean, we were still kind of sandy and messy from the beach and all, but after a cocktail or two at some pretty waterfront bar in Little Venice, it's not like we even noticed or cared.

In fact, I no longer cared about much of anything.

I no longer cared about my parents' divorce.

I no longer cared about moving.

I no longer cared about the fact that I was about to cheat on Yannis.

I no longer cared about the fact that I was about to cheat on Yannis with someone I no longer cared about.

Because suddenly, with my head all light, and cloudy,

and woozy, and with the music blaring so loud, and with Levi dancing so close—it was all good.

In fact, it was better than good it was—

Luminous!

And brilliant!

And shiny, and warm, and sexy, and glamorous, and exciting and fun!

And then suddenly my mouth was on Levi's, and his tongue was in mine, and his hands were sliding down my body, and my eyes were closed, and then the room started spinning, which was totally cool at first because I thought we were spinning together, like two people who are so madly in love they just spin across rooms. But then when I opened them again, I saw it was still Levi, and I tried to remind myself how much I once liked him, how popular he is, and how cute. How lucky I was to be there in his arms. How no other girl in our school, no other girl ANYWHERE had ever made out with him in a club in Mykonos. Not even that stupid Penelope chick. Not anyone. And then I remembered how I saw Yannis talking and laughing with Maria by the harbor, how he whispered *S'agapo* to me, and how I was leaving soon so it's not like it mattered. How there's no such thing as love. Just people who like to pretend they're in love. When the truth is it's false and invisible and doesn't really exist.

And I convinced myself so well of these things that I just kept kissing him back. Closing my eyes again, blocking everything out, letting the room grow calm and quiet until it settled around us, knowing that <u>THIS</u> was real. That fleeting moments like this were the best you could ever really hope for.

And so we kept kissing—between drinks, between songs, even after the club closed and we found ourselves a small, secluded beach where we kissed some more. We kissed as the sun came up. We kissed as he told me he had to head back to his boat. We kissed as he promised to e-mail. We kissed one last time before I headed off to my ferry, where I bought a ticket, climbed aboard, and watched as his boat sailed away from the dock—pressing my forehead against the smudgy, scratched glass, and wondering what the hell I'd just done.

## CIRCLE IN THE SAND

**0 Comments:**

*August 11*
*Dear Mom—*
    *For your information, I <u>KNOW</u> you <u>SOLD</u> the house. I got it straight from my source. So I guess what's done is done, and there's nothing more I can do.*
    *I'm sorry things didn't work out with your boyfriend (sorry, but I don't remember his name). But what I really need to know is if this means Arizona's back on?*
    *Let me know—*
    *Love,*
    *Colby*

*August 11*
*Dear Dad,*

*I'm sorry I accused you of being engaged when you're not. I guess my source is not nearly as reliable as I thought.*

*See you in a few weeks.*

*(It feels weird to write that.)*

*Love,*

*Colby*


August 11
To: NatalieZee
From: ColbyCat
Re: The sordid truth

It's true.

My mom sold the house. What can I say?

Though I want to thank you for all of your efforts in trying to sabotage it from the start. Seriously, for that alone I will be eternally grateful.

And, not like it probably matters much anyway, I mean, after everything that's happened and all, but I still want you to know that I'm actually really grateful for a lot of things that you've done. And I'm sorry that I acted like such a BIG FNB. (I know you hate abbreviations, but did you really want me to spell that out?) Or better yet—A BIG CONFORMING RETARD—like you once said.

And yeah, believe it or not the whole thing with Levi was totally real. But in the end it just wasn't as great as you'd think. Okay, maybe YOU never thought it would be even close to great, but we all know I did.

Well, if you want, I'm thinking maybe we can get together when I get back in town, before my mom makes me move to Arizona. (Yup, you read it right, though I'll explain it in another e-mail, on another day.)

Ya'Sou—

Colby

*August 12*
*Dear Aunt Tally and Tassos,*
*I'm sorry that:*

1)  *I made you worry.*
2)  *I didn't tell you I was going to Mykonos.*
3)  *I asked you to lie to Yannis.*
4)  *I broke the one and only house rule.*
5)  *My parents forced me on you and made you take me in, thereby wrecking your calm, tranquil, peaceful life.*
6)  *Etc. (I mean, I'm sure there's much more to be sorry for—but I'm hoping you'll accept a blanket apology for all of the infractions I may have missed.)*

*Just know that I'm really, really sorry.*
*Love,*
*Colby*

August 12
To: AmandaStar
From: ColbyCat

Re: summer lovin!

Hey Amanda,

Just responding to your e-mail, and thought I'd tell you that those pictures of you and Jenna and Penelope and Casey at the beach were really cute.

And to answer your questions:

—Yes, it was fun seeing Levi.

—And, yes those are real, live, alcoholic cocktails we're drinking in those pictures he sent you. There's no age limit here, so you can pretty much do whatever you want.

Anyway, I'll be home by the end of the month, but I'm not sure if I'll be going back to Harbor or not, since as you may or may not know, my mom sold the house, and I have no idea where I'll end up.

Okay, well, take care, and thanks for writing—

Colby

August 12

To: Levi501

From: ColbyCat

Re: party pics

Hey Levi,

Thanks for sending those pics. I forgot all about that one bar, though I definitely remember those blue drinks we both had! I think I might still be feeling it—just kidding! (Well, kind of.)

To answer your question, I'll be back on August 31, but

after that, I really don't know where I'll be since my mom sold the house, and I'm not sure where we'll be moving.

Anyway, it was good to see you too—

Enjoy the rest of the summer!

Colby

*August 12*

~~Dear Yannis,~~

~~I know you don't want to talk to me, so I'll just keep this brief and say that I'm sorry.~~

~~I'm really, really sorry.~~

~~Though I have to admit that I'm not really sure what I'm apologizing for, and I just wish you'd talk to me long enough to tell me, so then maybe I could try to explain.~~

~~I'll be here until the end of the month, in case you change your mind about seeing me.~~

~~Colby~~

~~P.S. It would have been really nice if you had told me where you lived, or maybe even invited me over so I'd know where to send this stupid letter. I guess you didn't really **S'AGAPO** me like you said! And no way am I asking Tally and/or Tassos for your address!~~

## CRUEL SUMMER

August 13

That's right, CRUEL SUMMER is back, but only long enough to say good-bye. After a brief period of sunshine, the clouds have moved in and the forecast shows nothing but gloom and doom from here on, my friends.

Though maybe it's just another sign that the end of summer is near, that my time in Tinos is over, and that I'll soon be heading home—wherever that turns out to be . . .

So, thanks to those of you who took the time to stop by, read, and/or comment me.

I really do appreciate it.

Love,

Colby

## COLBY'S JOURNAL FOR DESPERATE TIMES WHEN SHE'S FEELING REALLY DESPERATE

August 14

So yesterday, just after I signed off from my stupid, depressing, loser blog I was on my way home, basically dragging my feet and alternating between hating myself and feeling sorry for myself, when I decided to quit acting like such a pathetic little baby, and just go to the hotel, find Yannis, and get to the bottom of things once and for all.

I mean, in just two and a half weeks I'll be going home anyway, most likely never to return, so what does it really matter if I make a fool of myself, say something stupid, and/or end up looking like the world's biggest dork? It's not like anyone at home will ever know, so it's not like I had anything to lose.

Besides, I just couldn't bear the idea of returning to

California and leaving things the way they were—messy, unfinished, just hanging. I mean, if Yannis had dumped me for Maria, then I really wanted to hear it from him. And if he dumped me for some other reason, then I needed to know that too.

It's like, the whole thing was just so sudden, and unexpected, I guess I needed to make sense of it. Because according to both Tally and Tassos, he never even came by the house that night.

Which means they never had to lie to him.

Which also means there's no way he could've known about me, Levi, and Mykonos.

Which means, whatever happened, happened because of HIM.

It also means that technically, I'd been dumped well before I even got on that boat.

I just didn't realize it at the time.

And once I had that all straight in my head, I gave myself full permission to stop beating myself up, to stop feeling so guilty about everything, since in the end, it really didn't matter anyway. Apparently I was free and single, I just didn't know it.

But even though shirking all of the blame did make me feel better, it was pretty short-lived. I guess because it also left me with the one, ugly, undisputable truth—

I'd been dumped for the Greek vixen otherwise known as Maria.

And even though the thought of that made me feel completely nauseous and sick, I still needed to have it confirmed. I needed to be able to face the truth so I could file it away and move on. I mean, since my summer already had a beginning and middle, I knew it was time to give it an end.

But if I'm going to be <u>COMPLETELY</u> honest, then I also have to admit the slightly embarrassing truth of how part of me just really needed to see him again—just one last time, before I went away and ended our story for good. I guess I just wanted to make sure that we really were truly and completely over. And to get myself some closure if it turned out we were.

So instead of going home, I grabbed a taxi and headed straight for his hotel, thinking it was early enough that he'd probably still be working, and hopefully not late enough that he'd be engaging in something horrible and heartbreaking like entertaining Maria by the pool, in the same way he'd done with me.

So after I paid the driver, I climbed out of the car and just stood there, squinting at this sprawling, dusty, chaotic construction site that seemed to just go on forever, since the hotel is built bungalow style as opposed to high-rise.

And not really knowing where to start, I just walked right up to a group of construction workers, cleared my throat, and said, *"Poo ee neh Yannis?"* Which to my understanding meant, "Where is Yannis?" But when I was greeted by a series of shrugs followed by elbow nudges and laughter, I started to get a little concerned that I might've gotten it confused with another Greek phrase.

But then this old guy came up, grabbed my elbow, and led me to the other side of the hotel, where he walked into a room and shouted, *"Ela! Yannis!"* Then he shook his head and laughed as he walked away.

At this point I would love to be able to write that Yannis turned, took one look at me, and pulled me into his arms, holding me tight, refusing to let go. But that's the stuff of romance novels and sappy late-night movies, not real life. Because the truth is, he took one long, lingering look, then turned back around and continued his work.

I stood there, taking in his tan, muscled back that was dripping with sweat, his strong defined arms, their muscles bulging and popping as he hammered a nail, the cutoff jeans that Amanda would totally make fun of (but that's only because Amanda's an idiot), and my throat was so hot and constricted, and my heart felt so heavy and sad, that I closed my eyes and willed him to look at me, having no idea what I'd say if he did.

I mean, what do you say to the guy you just might have loved if only you hadn't been so shallow, so unsure of yourself, so afraid of letting him know? How do you explain how having the approval of people who weren't really your friends, far outweighed anything you just might've felt? And how because of all that, you ran off to Mykonos to meet up with someone who turned out to be so completely and totally unworthy?

But then I reminded myself how I didn't actually need any of those words.

Because, it's not like he knew any of that.

Which meant there was no reason for me to confess, since it was now up to him to confess.

Because the fact is, he was hanging in the port with Maria, long before my ship even sailed.

He was the one laughing and talking and having a great old time.

He was the one who allowed her to touch his arm, as she leaned in to kiss his cheek.

Right there in broad daylight.

Right where I could see.

When just the night before he'd said he'd be working all through siesta, which was why he couldn't go to the beach with me.

Which was pretty much the ultimate final thing that made me decide to get on that boat in the first place.

So if anyone had any explaining to do, it was he.

I opened my eyes, cleared my throat, and said, "Hey, Yannis? Um, hello? Are you trying to ignore me?" (Talk about stating the obvious.) Then I continued to stand there, watching as he pounded the heck out of another nail, acting as though I didn't exist.

So then I cleared my throat again and went, "Hey, Yannis, listen, I know you're mad, but I also know you can hear me, so I'd really appreciate it if you could just stop hammering, turn around, and give me the courtesy of ten minutes of your time."

He kept pounding.

"Five minutes?" I said, knowing I was in no position to bargain since I was on his turf and would end up settling for whatever I could get.

More pounding.

"Fine. One minute and thirty seconds, final offer," I said, unaware I'd been holding my breath until he set down the hammer and I gulped some air.

And even though he still refused to look at me, I knew I had to take advantage of the moment while it lasted, and with no time to waste, I took another deep breath and dove in. "Why won't you talk to me?" I asked, my eyes searching the back of his head, willing him to turn around and acknowledge me once and for all. "Why'd you stop coming by and answering my calls? Are you mad at me? And if so, why? I mean, *WHAT HAPPENED?* Because I think I deserve an explanation. Because you can't just string someone along, whisper *I love you,* then act like they don't even exist," I said, immediately growing all red faced and shaky, my heart crashing against my chest, as my mind raced back to the I LOVE YOU part, which I tortured myself by playing over and over again.

And when he finally turned to look at me, my eyes went straight for his, hoping to find them soft, warm, and caring, the same way I'd left them last week. Only now they were different, changed, alien even. Their cold, hard detachment providing all the answer I needed.

And then he shrugged. And then he shook his head and said, "Listen, Colby, you're leaving in what? Two weeks?"

"Two and a half," I said, my stomach going all twisty and turvy and awful.

"Okay, so we had some fun, but now it's over. You go back to your life, I go back to mine." He shrugged. "Another summer is finished."

"So that's it?" I asked, my eyes stinging, not expecting to be brushed off and discarded so easily.

*I mean, who was this guy? Did I ever even know him? Was I really so naïve to think I was anything more than just some stupid summer fling?*

He shrugged.

"So that's why you decided to dump me?" I said, amazed that I could even speak with the way my throat felt so hot and constricted. "Because the summer's over? I mean, no long good-bye at the port? No postcards or e-mails? You just go cold turkey? Decide to get a head start and dump me two weeks early, without notice?" And then I tried to laugh, tried to make it sound as though I cared a lot less than it seemed. But in the end I didn't fool anyone, because it came out sounding really false and lame.

But even after all that, even after my whole tirade, all he could manage in response was a shrug.

Which turned out to be a really bad choice.

I narrowed my eyes, placed my hands on my hips, took a deep breath, and went full steam ahead. "Because I'm actually kind of wondering if it's maybe something else? I'm actually wondering if it might have something to do with the fact that I saw you at the port with Maria," I said, the sweat transferring from my palms to my shorts, not sure where I was headed, but unable (unwilling?) to stop. "I saw you guys together, by the harbor, at the fish market, the same day you couldn't be bothered to go to the beach with me because you said you had to work straight through siesta. And then the next thing I know, you stop coming over, won't take my calls, and pretty much ignore me."

And while I was waiting for a response, he did the strangest thing—he just shook his head and laughed.

<u>LAUGHED!</u>

And I was so surprised by his reaction it took me a moment or two to get that it wasn't the kind of laugh that was inviting me to join in. It was more the kind that was directed at <u>US.</u> How we were standing there together, in that room, sharing a moment that was so small it couldn't possibly be anything other than funny. As though the two of us together, was so unworthy, so insignificant, it became a big fat joke.

And when he finally stopped laughing, he said, "It does not really matter anymore, does it?"

I stood there, staring down at my suntanned feet, my eyes focused on my peach-colored polish, my silver toe ring, and the tiny star tattoo my mom still doesn't know about. Because even though I've always known we would end, I never imagined it would hurt like this.

So after biting my lip so hard I practically drew blood, after blinking my eyes so many times I finally chased away the tears, I brushed my hair off my face, tucked it behind my ears, and said, "You're right, none of it matters anymore. So . . ."

I wanted to finish with something light, and pithy, maybe even sarcastic. Something that would let him know I was right there with him, that I thought it was funny too, that I was perfectly okay, despite all outward appearances.

But in the end, I didn't say anything. Because my

throat was searing again, my vision was blurred, and since I couldn't afford to let him see me like that, I turned and ran straight out of that horrible, dusty room—and all the way home.

Or at least back to my summer home.

Tally and Tassos's home.

I guess I'm not really sure where home is anymore.

## CRUEL SUMMER

August 17

Okay, I know that just a few days ago I swore the blog was history, over, kaput! But since there's still two weeks left of summer, I figured I may as well see it all the way through to the bitter end. Partly because it gives me something to do, but mostly because I'm turning over a new leaf, so to speak, which means I am newly committed to finishing the things that I start.

Also, I'm determined to hold my position as Petros's #1 customer. Which pretty much requires me to spend some serious time (and money!) right here in his café!

And even though I know it probably sounds crazy, especially since I spent the entire first month pretty much hating every single thing about this place (I mean, Tinos, not the café), now that it's almost time for me to leave, I'm actually kind of sad.

So with that in mind, I've been spending less time in my room, and more time at the beach and exploring the island, sometimes with Tally and Tassos, sometimes just out on my own, taking pictures of everything I experience—a few of which you can see here:

1) This is my still-missing kitten, Mr. Holly Golightly. He is a black male with blue eyes and a white streak across his forehead. He likes to be petted, but only a little, because mostly he likes to run free. So if you find him (and I hope that you do because he's been missing for more than a week—and I'm <u>VERY</u> worried about him) please pick him up gently (but don't hold him too tight, because he will fight like hell to get away), and bring him straight to Petros's Internet café, or my aunt Tally's gift shop (located at the very end of the same street).

2) This is the first vase I made that didn't collapse! It only took me about one hundred and eighty-five tries to get to this point—and trust me, that is only a <u>SLIGHT</u> exaggeration. And the only reason I even made it this far is because Tassos is like the world's most patient, kind, knowledgeable, and generous (did I say <u>PATIENT</u>?) teacher. And later today, he's going to teach me how to glaze it and fire it, and I can hardly wait to see how it turns out. (And if it's any good, I'll post a picture!)

3) This is a pair of earrings I made last night with Tally, while we sat outside on the terrace, eating this amazing rice pudding (with a name I can't pronounce much less spell but which has a direct

translation of "rice milk") as we watched the sunset, listened to the Beatles, and made jewelry. And even though I really like the way these turned out, I'm thinking I might give them to a friend of mine, because as Tally always says—"You should always give what you want for yourself." Whatever, I just hope my friend likes them too.

4) This is a picture of a place called Exobourgo, which is this amazing mountain that a friend of mine once took me to, and it's so pretty I decided to go back on my own. It only takes around fifteen or twenty minutes to hike all the way to the top, and once you're up there, the view is amazing! Seriously, you can see all of Tinos and some of the other Cyclades islands as well. It's really pretty magical, and if you don't believe me, then check out #5.

5) See? Is that not the most amazing view EVER? That was taken from the very top of Exobourgo, and I have to say I've never seen anything like it back home! Look how calm that turquoise water is, how the distant houses resemble shiny little sugar cubes, and how the surrounding islands look like glimmering brown jewels! It's so amazing I wish you could see for yourself, but for now, this will have to do!

6) Okay, since the rest are just pictures of landscapes, I'm not going to identify every single location shot. Besides, if you've been following this blog at all,

then you should be very familiar with dirt, rocks, and geraniums by now. I know I am!

Enjoy—
Colby

August 17
To: NatalieZee
From: ColbyCat
Re: Arizona?
Hey Nat,

I wish I could answer your question, but I can't. Because the truth is I have no idea whether I'll be going back to Harbor, moving to Arizona, or enrolling in Cyber School (and no, I have no idea what that is, but I heard my parents mention it once during one of their many fights, so I can't go ruling it out). Because as my mom recently explained, she had no idea the house would sell that quickly, and to quote her directly, she is now—"Doing my best, meeting with agents, frantically searching and putting the word out for a nice, affordable place for us to live, so DON'T go accusing me of not looking, or caring, or taking this seriously, Colby!"

She also assures me that she will let me know the moment she secures something, so I really need to "stop bugging her, stop second-guessing her, and just let her handle it."

Whatever.

Anyway, it's really nice of you and your mom to offer to let me use your address so I can stay at Harbor, but I really don't want to impose, or get you guys in trouble or anything, and besides, I still don't even know if I'll need it. But thanks anyway.

Also, to answer your question, <u>NO,</u> Amanda has not offered to let me use her address. So, feel free to draw your own conclusions.

Okay, Petros is closing up shop for siesta—so, gotta go!
Colby


## COLBY'S JOURNAL FOR DESPERATE TIMES

August 19

So yesterday started like any other day. I woke up, I ate breakfast, I showered, I checked all around the house, both inside and out, to see if Holly had come back (he hadn't) and then I headed out the door and down to the café, taking my usual route, and enjoying the nice, sunny, slightly windy day, but also thinking how it wasn't really so different from any other day I'd spent here. I mean, I actually remember thinking those very words.

But as it turns out, I couldn't have been more wrong.

Because by the time I'd made it to the café and was reaching for the door handle, I was no longer thinking about much of anything, no longer noticing my surroundings, because I was back on autopilot, expecting just to go inside, say hi to Petros, order my frappe, and sit at my usual table where I'd log on and start blogging away.

Which is why I was so surprised to find the door locked.

So surprised that I immediately tried to open it again. Only it was still locked. And even after I'd taken a step back and gazed at the sign in the window, clearly seeing how it read CLOSED and <u>NOT</u> OPEN, it was as though I still couldn't quite make my eyes believe it. So I cupped my hands around my face and peered inside. And even though I didn't see anyone in there, that didn't stop me from tapping hard on the window, and yelling for Petros to come out from the back room and unlock the door and let me in already.

And even after he still didn't answer, I just continued to stand there, gazing inside, wondering if it was some kind of holiday I wasn't aware of.

But after awhile, when my laptop bag started carving a nice, deep wedge into my shoulder as I gawked at the locked and empty room, I finally decided to just let it go and was turning to leave when I spotted Yannis, coming out of a shop, just a few doors away.

Well, my heart started racing, and my palms started to sweat, and I felt so suddenly panicked (not to mention suddenly ridiculous for feeling so suddenly panicked) that I looked all around, frantically searching for somewhere to hide, someplace I could duck into, where he wouldn't see me.

Only there was no place. Because I was trapped in plain sight, and he was heading straight for me. And left with no other option, I took a deep breath and ordered myself to just grow up, relax, and deal with it already. And just as I was doubting I could even do that, it occurred to me that he probably wasn't coming toward <u>ME</u>

at all. He was probably just trying to get to the end of the street, a street through which no fault of his own, I happened to be on.

So then just as he got that much closer, I turned really quickly and started walking away, the soles of my sandals slapping the pavement as though I had somewhere to be.

And even after he started calling my name, going, "Colby! Hey! Please wait!" I just kept going. Even when I started to feel pretty winded, I pushed on. Because no way was I going to stop to see what he wanted. I mean, I'd barely gotten through our last little meeting, so I definitely wasn't up for a do-over.

But apparently, all that construction work has left Yannis in way better shape than me, because the next thing I knew, his hand was on my shoulder, and he was pretty much forcing me to stop, turn, and face him. And when I finally gave up and gave in, when I finally turned and looked, his face seemed so sad and so serious, my heart skipped a few beats.

Because in that exact moment I <u>KNEW</u> he was about to apologize. I was <u>POSITIVE</u> he was going to take it all back, everything he'd said, including the horrible way he'd laughed at me/us. I mean, it was so obvious, the proof was right there before me, all I had to do was look into his eyes and see it.

And the only thing left was for me to decide whether or not to accept.

But instead he said, "Colby, I'm so sorry, but Petros is dead."

I stared at him, for what felt like the longest time, but was probably only a few seconds, and then I said, "No he's not." Then I started back down the street.

Though I'd barely taken two steps before he was right on top of me again, and this time he put both hands on my shoulders, looked me right in the eye, and said, "Colby, Petros had a heart attack. He didn't make it."

But I just shook my head and pulled away. "You're wrong. I just saw him yesterday, and for your information he was totally fine," I said, trying to understand why he'd even attempt to do something so cruel. I mean, what did he hope to get out of it? Why was he trying so hard to hurt me?

But even though he was shaking his head, saying, "Colby, please listen, it's true. They were even going to airlift him to Athens but he did not make it. I'm very sorry to have to tell you this," I just turned back around and headed home.

And when I saw Tally and Tassos that night, they confirmed it was true. But even though they fussed all over me, asking if I was all right, insisting that it's perfectly okay to cry, I just couldn't. I mean, it's not like I knew Petros all that well. It's not like I'd let myself get all attached. He was just some guy who provided coffee and an Internet connection. That's it, nothing more.

Just like Yannis was a guy I once skinny-dipped with.

And Holly was just some cat I rescued until he was well enough to go off on his own.

And if at any time in the past, I was careless enough to

think that any of those things had any more value than that, well, I was over it now. Because the truth is, it's just a whole lot better to not let yourself get too involved with anyone, or anything.

Because in the end—everything comes to an end.

*August 21*
*Dear Dad,*

*I don't know if I told you this but today they're having a funeral for ~~a friend of mine~~ this person I met here. But I'm going to the beach instead since it's not like I knew him all that well anyway, and since I only have a little over a week left, I figure I may as well spend it at the beach. I'm not sure why I even just wrote that, except maybe it's because summer's almost over, and I really don't have much else to say.*

*Okay, well, see you soon-ish.*

*Love,*

*Colby*

*P.S. Oh yeah, I meant to ask you if there's still enough room for me, for when I come visit you? I mean, now that your girlfriend is living with you. Let me know.*

*August 21*
*Dear Mom,*

*I would really appreciate it if the next time we talk on the phone you could stop telling me stuff about Dad, since I figure he can probably just tell me himself if he really wants me to know, and honestly, at this exact moment, the only news I really want to hear from you is where I'll be living when I get back. Really, that's* it. I mean, I want to hear how you're doing as well, don't get me wrong, but I definitely don't want to hear about anything outside of those two things.

Sorry if that sounds a little harsh, but I just don't know how else to say it.

Love,
Colby

P.S. ~~This guy I met here recently died and his funeral is to-day, but I think I'm going to go to the beach instead.~~ Sorry, ignore that! I don't even know why I wrote it.

August 21
Dear Nat,

I'm writing you this postcard because the guy who owned the Internet café (Petros) died of a heart attack and his funeral is today, which means the Internet café is closed. So I just thought I'd write instead. And then I guess I'll go to the beach, since I don't really see the point in going to the funeral of someone who I barely knew and wasn't actually like a true friend of mine or anything.

Still no word on where I'll be living—can you even believe it?

Okay, well, see you soon—
Colby

August 21
Dear Amanda,

I don't know if you've tried to e-mail me or not but I don't have Internet access right now since the guy who owned the café (Petros, you know the one whose mustache you made fun of?), well, he had a heart attack and died suddenly with no warning *whatsoever. Which means his shop is closed—so no more blogging or e-mailing for a while, maybe even forever, I really don't know. Though it's definitely closed for today since it's his funeral, but I'm just going to spend the day at the beach instead.*

*Okay, well, I just thought I'd let you know why I'm not answering back in case you do/did try to message me.*

*C U soon—*

*Colby*

*August 21*

*Dear Tally and Tassos,*

*I'm going to the beach today, so I probably won't see you until later this evening. Have a good one.*

*Love,*

*Colby*

### COLBY'S JOURNAL FOR DESPERATE TIMES WHEN SHE HAS NO IDEA WHY SHE FEELS SO DESPERATE

August 21

Hard as it is to believe, today marks the first time I dragged my journal out of the house and down to the beach. But then again this is also one of the first times I've gone to the beach by myself. And I'm not even sure why I chose to do this today, except for the fact that I felt like being alone. Though I was sick of being alone in my room, since I've wasted far too much time in there already, so I figured I may as well go someplace warm, beautiful, and sunny, but also quiet.

And it's funny how sitting here on my towel writing this kind of makes me feel like I'm keeping up my routine, since I'm used to spending my mornings writing in my blog, and sending e-mails, and postcards and letters, even though it was always at the café, never here, and always while I was sipping frappe, and not from a water bottle. But still, somehow it makes me feel like everything's still normal, that my routine is still useful, and that nothing's really changed.

Even though I'm really not delusional enough to actually believe any of that.

## Much Later:

Okay, just after I wrote that, I started feeling all choked up. Seriously, my throat started aching, and my eyes started stinging, only this time there was nothing I could do to stop it. And even though I tried to fight it, even though I tried to hold it all in, it wasn't long before the tears started pouring down my face. So I got up from my towel and ran into the sea, where I dove under the water and swam out as far as I could, my eyes shut tight against the stinging saltiness, blind to everything in front of me, but not even caring. And when I couldn't hold my breath any longer, I popped back up, gasping and taking huge gulps of air before ducking back under and continuing on, swimming as fast and far as I could, my arms and legs aching from the strain, until they became rubbery, weak, and useless. And when I finally stopped, I allowed myself to surrender to the sea, just float on my back with my eyes closed tightly against the sun, the heat drying my face, leaving grainy salt trails across my cheeks. Shutting down the thoughts in my head, refusing to tune into anything more than the gentle slap and sway of the water, until my fingers and toes were all pruney. Until the threat of emotions had passed.

Then later, as I made my way toward shore, my stomach dropped to my knees when I saw Tally sitting next to my towel. But I just took a deep breath and kept moving, putting one foot in front of the other until I was standing directly before her. Then acting as though everything was perfectly fine and okay, I smiled and said, "Hey, Tally, what's up?" Then I twisted my hair into a long spiral, squeezing it tightly between the palms of my hands, watching as seawater poured through the ends.

She smiled and shrugged, then mumbled something about it being a great day for the beach, and my stomach leapt from my knees to my throat when I saw how I'd left my journal lying right there on my towel, all propped open and ready for anyone interested enough to read.

And just as I started to grab it, frantic to think what she might've seen, I remembered that this was Tally, my peace-loving, privacy-allowing aunt who would never even consider peeking at someone else's diary.

Which pretty much makes her the exact opposite of her sister/my mom who would dive right in without a second thought.

So instead I just nudged it aside with my foot, as though it held no real significance or value, then I sat down beside her and admired my tan as I splayed my legs out before me (well, at least until I got to my toenails which were desperately in need of fresh paint). And since she was just sitting there beside me, not saying a word, I turned to her and said, "Where's Tassos?" Even though I figured he was probably busy working at his studio. But then I didn't really care about the answer—I just wanted to plug up the silence.

But she said, "At the house, getting ready."

And just as I was about to ask—*getting ready for what?* I REMEMBERED. So I shut my mouth and left it at that.

"I just thought I'd stop by and sit with you for a while. I hope that's okay?" she said, giving me a cautious look, which made me feel kind of bad, but still I just shrugged. "You're leaving soon, and I feel like we didn't get to spend enough time together." She laughed. "Crazy, huh? We've lived together nearly three months, but somehow it just flew by." She smiled.

I glanced at her and nodded, then I focused back on my toes, partly because I didn't trust the awful way my throat was starting to feel again, but mostly because I was wondering how she was going to segue this little conversation into that of Petros's funeral, mentioning how weird it was that neither of us were there. Especially me.

But instead she just sighed and said, "I hope it wasn't all bad, Colby, your time here, I mean. I know my lifestyle isn't quite what you had in mind for your summer vacation."

I just shrugged, because while the majority of it was indisputably bad, it's not like it was her fault.

"I have to admit, when your mom called to ask if I'd take you in for the summer I was more than a little surprised." She laughed. "But then she explained about the divorce, and I thought it would be a good break for you. Because believe me, I've been there."

I looked at her, wondering what the heck she was getting at. I mean, how could she have "been there" when the only reason Grandma was single was because Grandpa died? How could she know how horrible it is when your parents wake up one morning and mutually decide that from that moment on they'll totally hate each other?

"I was married." She smiled, answering the question I hadn't yet asked. "A long time ago, right before I moved here, it only lasted a year, and you were just a tiny baby, which is why you probably don't know."

"Was it horrible?" I asked, preparing to hear a really juicy, if not tragic, tale.

But she just shrugged. "Not really." And when she saw my expression she laughed and said, "Not all endings are bad, Colby. Just like not all endings are happy. Some endings—just—are." She shrugged. "But no matter what happens, you always come out okay."

And when I looked at her I thought:

*More peace and love crap coming right up!*

But then I felt immediately guilty for thinking that, so I just scooped up a handful of sand, cupped it in the center of my palm, and watched as it slipped through my fingers, landing right back where it started, settling into place as though it'd never been disturbed. And after it was quiet for so long I just couldn't take it anymore, I said, "Well, maybe that worked out all fine and well for you, but just so you know, my parents' divorce isn't even final yet, and my dad's already living with someone, and my mom sold the house and has no idea where we'll go because she's too busy obsessing over my dad's new girlfriend, and they just continue along like that, happily screwing up all of our lives, and there's nothing I can do about it! Not one damn thing I can do to change it! So yeah, I guess you're right, I just have to accept it because it is what it is, but that doesn't mean I'm going to be okay, I mean you can't <u>PROVE</u> that because there's just no guarantee—" But even though I was poised and ready to go on and on and on, in the end, I cut it off there, since I couldn't guarantee I wouldn't do something completely embarrassing like start crying right in front of her, or worse.

But Tally just shook her head and said, "You're right, Colby. You had no choice, and everything you're going through is out of your control. But what I really meant to say is that even though it's true that all of these things have happened to you, the fact is, you've lived through it, and you're still fine. And you'll continue to be fine. Your mom will find somewhere for you to live, and you'll be fine. And if you have to go to a new school, it won't be long before you learn your way around, make new friends, and you'll be fine again. You'll meet your dad's new girlfriend, and whether or not you like her really doesn't matter, because either way, you'll still be fine. Life brings nothing *but* change, Colby. Our job is to make the necessary adjustments, so we can continue to be fine."

But she'd barely gotten to the end of her speech before I was already shaking my head. "Um, excuse me for saying this, but how would you even know? I mean, it's not like your life embraces change," I said, thinking how she'd moved to a place that's so unbelievably stagnant and slow it seems like nothing's changed for over a century. "I mean, you buy your eggs off an old lady on a donkey, you buy your fish off a boat in the harbor, you don't even have a computer, much less a TV, not to mention how you and Tassos basically keep to the same routine, day in and day out, come rain, shine, or Meltemi wind. So, not to be rude or anything, but in light of all that, I really don't get how you can possibly claim to be such an authority on change. I mean, you're practically living in a time warp!"

But even though I was poised for a fight, Tally just laughed. "You're right," she said, her legs crossed, her hands folded in her lap, her face as serene as the Buddha statue she keeps in her garden. "And that's exactly why I moved here at first. I was searching for someplace stable, steady, and calm. And you know what I got? More change. Maybe not as intense as before, but still, it ebbs and flows here just like any other life. Sometimes the change is small, sometimes it's not, but in the end, you always come out better, wiser, or maybe just okay. And if you're lucky, you get all three."

And that's when I rolled my eyes.

I know I shouldn't have done it, but it's not like I could help it, because as much as I'd grown to like her, as much as I'd learned to tolerate our colossal differences, sometimes she was just so dang full of it.

I watched as she calmly got up, grabbed her keys, and then looked at me as she said, "The trick is to learn to see with your heart, not with your eyes, Colby."

And when I called after her, to ask where she was going, she just smiled and said, "I have a funeral to attend."

*August 21*
*Dear Tally and Tassos,*
    *The mailman just delivered your new* <u>COMPUTER!</u>
    *I left the box in the kitchen, next to the table.*
    *Is this for real?*
    *Let me know if you need me to show you how to use it!*
    *Colby*

## COLBY'S JOURNAL

August 22

The second I heard Tally's jeep drive away, I got up from my towel and ran after her, waving my arms and yelling into the cloud of dust she'd left behind, but it was too late, she'd already gone. So I ran back down to the beach, shoved everything in my bag, and headed back up the road and all the way home. Ignoring the searing pain in my side as I gasped for air and pushed on, concentrating on nothing more than changing out of my wet bathing suit, and into something appropriate enough to wear to Petros's funeral.

Because the second Tally was gone, I knew she was right. It was time for me to stop worrying about how everything APPEARS. To stop worrying about how it will all END. And learn to enjoy what I have—for as long as I have it.

And just as I was about to walk through the door, a delivery truck pulled into the drive, and some guy climbed out holding this big huge box in his hands that he asked me to sign for, and I nearly fell over when I saw it contained a computer.

But it's not like I had much time to really stop and gawk since I knew the funeral had probably already started, and I didn't want to be any more late than I already was, since the Greeks take their traditions very seriously.

So after taking a really quick shower, and twisting my clean, wet hair back into a bun, I threw on a black dress, slipped on some sandals, and flew out the door, running all the way down to the church where I really, really hoped it was being held, since in this case, being wrong meant I had 699 others to choose from. And when I slipped inside, the room was so dim and cloudy with incense it took awhile for my eyes to adjust, and even though I immediately spotted Tally and Tassos somewhere in the middle, I decided to just hang in the back and try not to attract any more attention than I already had.

I leaned against the back wall, listening as the priests in

their long, ornate robes chanted an endless string of words that sounded completely unfamiliar, as my eyes searched the crowd of mourners, seeing Petros's son, Stavros, struggling to remain stoic even though he was clearly overcome with grief, his arm wrapped around a small, pale, trembling woman I figured to be his mother. And after seeing the guy who works at the bank, nodding at the guy who runs the gyros stand, and acknowledging and recognizing a whole host of others, I realized that as much as I'd tried to fight it, I'd somehow become a part of this community.

Then I froze, I mean seriously I could not blink, breathe, or move when I saw Yannis standing next to Maria. But it only lasted a second. Because even though seeing them together made my stomach pang with this deep terrible ache, in the end I forced my eyes to look away, reminding myself that I was there to honor Petros, not to revisit my long list of regrets.

After the ceremony, everyone filed out of the church and headed for the cemetery, and I was standing by the door, waiting for Tally and Tassos to catch up, when Yannis came right up beside me and whispered, "Walk with me." Not like a question, though not quite an order either, I guess it was more like a suggestion.

So I did. I headed out the door and walked alongside him, neither one of us saying a word, just following the flow of the crowd, until he grabbed my hand, pulled me against the wall, and let everyone pass, until only we remained.

Then he looked at me and said, "Are you okay?"

His eyes were on mine, and his face showed such warmth and concern and care, that I just couldn't help it, I burst out laughing.

Not that I thought it was funny or anything, since obviously it was a completely normal question under the circumstances (unlike my response, which was anything but normal). But after listening to that little speech of Tally's at the beach, somehow it all just seemed kind of funny. Because the fact was, until he'd asked, I didn't even realize that I was okay. That, come to think of it, I'd been okay all along. That even though I was still really sad about Petros, and still really worried about my future, and still beyond annoyed with my parents, and still quite possibly choosing the wrong friends over the right ones, I, Colby Catherine Cavendish, was still okay. And there was a pretty good chance I'd remain that way, no matter what.

That with a little effort, most of the stupid mistakes I'd made could be fixed. And as for the rest? Well, I'd just learn to deal. And for some stupid reason, that I can't really explain, all of that made me feel like laughing, even though it was obviously NOT the response he was after (nor was it appropriate conduct from someone who just came from a funeral). But I guess it also felt good to laugh again. It'd been far too long since the last time.

And like always with laughing, it wasn't long before Yannis joined in too, though it was pretty obvious it was more of a hesitant, confused laugh, like he wasn't exactly sure why he was participating, but figured, well, what the hell?

So when I finally calmed down, I looked him right in the eyes and said, "Oh my God, you're anonymous aren't you?" Even though I hadn't realized I knew until exactly that moment.

He nodded.

So I said, "And that's why you dumped me, because you read about my trip to Mykonos." And as I watched him nod again, I couldn't believe how it'd taken me so long to figure it out. Though I still had no idea how he even knew about my blog in the first place, since it's not like I ever told him about it. But I also knew it didn't matter. What did matter was the way I'd hurt him. So I looked at him and said, "I'm sorry." Which seemed a little inadequate, so I added, "But it's not what you think because nothing happened, I swear. I mean, I'm not going to lie, we kissed—" I glanced at him briefly, then quickly looked away, the pain in his eyes being too much to bear. "But that's it. *Really*—"

I lowered my gaze and focused on my feet, wishing I could go back and change things, yet knowing I could only move forward. So I took a deep breath and said, "I guess I was just so afraid of what I might lose, of what I might be missing out on, that I forgot to enjoy what I have. And I somehow believed that by pushing you away and rejecting everything here, I could reclaim my old life, the one I left behind. Only it didn't work. It just left me feeling sad and awful and empty inside."

When I looked up again his eyes were on mine, and it took everything I had not to look away.

"Is he your boyfriend?" he asked, his eyes narrowed.

I shook my head. "I don't even like him."

"And nothing happened?"

I gazed at him and swallowed hard, hating the words but knowing I had to say them. "We kissed, but that's all."

My hands were shaking, my palms were sweating, and my lips were pressed so tight it hurt, and when I glimpsed his expression, just seconds before he shook his head and looked away, I knew it was useless, I knew it was over.

But then he shrugged and said, "I'm sorry too."

I froze, wondering if he had his own confession to make, something about Maria. And not really sure if I wanted the details, but knowing he deserved equal time, I asked, "What are you sorry for?"

He shook his head. "It was a stupid game, pretending to be anonymous. I should have told you. I just wanted to know you better. You always seem like you are keeping something back. You could have told me about your parents, and your friend coming to visit. Why did you keep it a secret?"

And even though it was a good, reasonable, valid question, that doesn't mean I had an answer. So I just shrugged and said, "Well, now you know. But how did you know, about the blog? I mean, is Petros another cousin?"

Yannis laughed. "He is a cousin of my cousin, but not a direct relation. I stopped by his café one day when you were in there, and I recognized you from the boat, but you didn't see me since you were too busy typing. And when I asked Petros about you, he told me about your blog, and I started reading it so that I could learn more about you. The only reason I showed up at the Fourth of July BBQ was so that I could meet you." He shrugged.

"So you were stalking me?" I asked, realizing that for someone who thought she knew all the answers, I really didn't know much of anything.

But he just laughed.

"And Maria?" I asked, still feeling that pang in my gut, despite everything he'd just told me.

But he just shook his head and slid along the wall, moving so close I could feel the warmth of his body, his breath on my cheek, as he looked at me and said, "The only reason I was in the port that day is because I was buying the flowers and food for our date. I'm not interested in Maria." His eyes searched my face. "Unfortunately, I'm still interested in you."

"Unfortunately?" I murmured, barely able to breathe as he brought his hand to my face, his fingers traveling along my temple, my cheekbone, stopping just long enough to tuck a loose strand of hair behind my ear, before returning to the curve of my chin.

"You're leaving." He shrugged, his eyes gazing right into mine, his fingers tilting my face toward his. "It's unfortunate."

"So what happens now?" I whispered, as he kissed the side of my neck, halfway between my ear and my necklace.

"We make the most of it," he said, his lips meeting mine.

We kissed. Right there, next to the whitewashed wall, smack in the middle of town, where anyone could see. Just clinging to each other, lost in our own little world, oblivious to everything around us, until an old woman walked by and *tsk'd*.

Actually, she muttered something under her breath as well. But even though I asked Yannis to translate, he just shook his head, and said I was better off not knowing. Then he grabbed my hand and led me to where another old woman was selling flowers from a basket hanging off the side of her donkey.

So of course I said, "Oh, you don't have to buy me flowers." Even though I was secretly thrilled that he was.

But he just laughed and said, "They're not for you, they're for Petros. Come on, it's a tradition."

By the time we made it to the cemetery, the ceremony was over, and everyone had moved on, so Yannis and I walked right up to the grave site, and I watched while he placed a single white rose on the grave and said a few words in Greek. Then I placed a pink rose beside his and said, "Thanks for being my friend. And thanks for giving me good advice and telling me to turn off my computer, go outside, and get a life. And thanks for pulling no punches and letting me know when you thought I was up to no good." I peeked at Yannis right after I said that, wondering if Petros had told him about the day I came back from Mykonos and how awful I looked and how I reeked of alcohol and sweat, but he was still gazing at the grave, so I took a deep breath and went on, "And thanks for that free frappe. I'll miss you."

And even though I thought I'd probably start crying the second that was out, I didn't. But not because I was embarrassed, or wanted to appear strong or cool in front of Yannis—I guess just knowing it was okay to show emotion made it no longer necessary to hide it.

And after saying good-bye to Petros, Yannis grabbed my hand and we headed into town, anxious to make up for all that lost time.

## CIRCLE IN THE SAND

August 25

I'm back! Thanks to Tally and Tassos who are now totally hooked into the new millennium and have finally gone wireless! Yipee! Which means I can now blog from the comfort of my room, the kitchen table, the couch, the terrace, wherever! And it's all because they said they wanted to keep in touch with me! And even though I don't doubt that to be true, I also happen to know that they're thinking of selling all the art and stuff they make in their own online store, which means they pretty much needed a computer to do that.

Anyway, you were probably a little confused when you saw the blog name, right? I know, I know, I just can't seem to stick with a title. I guess I tend to be a little fickle, somewhat flighty, and perhaps even just a tad bit impulsive (but those are only a few of my many, many quirks, I assure you). Though let me also assure you that "Circle in the Sand" is officially back and will hold at least until I leave on August 31, which unfortunately, is now just a few days away.

Yup, you read that right, I said UNFORTUNATELY. Because even though I spent the better part of the summer longing to be just about anywhere but here, wouldn't you know it, now that it's nearly time for me to leave, this has pretty much become the only place I want to be.

Still, the fact remains that my days here are few, and since I'm determined not to waste any more than I already have, I will keep it short and sweet and show you what I've been up to:

1) This is a picture of me and Yannis out on his cousin's boat. I thought I was teaching them how to wakeboard, until I discovered that they already knew how to wakeboard—way, WAY better than me.

2) That's me and Yannis lying on the beach, that very same day, after the wakeboarding instruction. Notice how wrecked and exhausted I look. That's what wiping out on the wakeboard, over and over again, will do to a person.

3) That's me and Yannis's cousin Nikos eating a sea

urchin that I caught! Seriously! I mean, I pricked my finger pretty badly when I picked it up, but still, it was awesome. That's right, believe it or not I've really learned to love them and I have no idea what I'm going to do when I go back home and I won't be able to eat them all the time anymore. But I guess, there's always frozen yogurt—which is something they don't have here!

4)  That's us, at the club, dancing. Blah, blah, blah, I know you've seen those same kind of shots like a thousand times already. So, moving on . . .

5)  Oops! Okay, again, another club picture of us drinking (non-alcoholic, I swear!) and hanging out in our usual booth. I like to think of it as the VIP booth, even though it's not.

6)  This is a photo of our (Yannis and my) favorite beach. Though the reason you can't see it very well is because it was taken at night, after the club, so it's pretty much just dark sand, darker water, and really dark sky.

7)  This is another picture of my cat, Mr. Holly Golightly, who has been missing for several weeks now. If you should find him, please, please pick him up gently (because he does NOT like to be cuddled or held for very long—and trust me, you do NOT want to get scratched!) and deliver him to Tally's Gift Shop located in the harbor front. I promise there will be a reward.

That's all for now!
Ciao!
Colby

August 26
To: AmandaStar
From: ColbyCat
Re: Wazup W/U & sandal guy?
Hey Amanda,

I got your e-mail, and just thought I'd let you know that SANDAL GUY has a name—it's YANNIS.

And just so you know, he also happens to be MY BOY-FRIEND.

And the only reason I didn't tell you this before is because I knew you'd make fun of both him and me. But now I no longer care about things like that, so there it is.

Feel free to forward this e-mail to the entire Harbor High School student body if that'll make you happy, since the truth is, I no longer care about stuff like that either.

Sincerely,
Colby

## CIRCLE IN THE SAND

**Blog Comments:**

**Anonymous said:**

It's so good to have you back!

**ColbyCat said:**

It's AMAZINGLY good to be back!

*August 26*

*Dear Mom and Dad,*

*Just so you know, I'm sending each of you a copy of this exact same letter so you don't have to freak out and arrange another conference call. I mean, if you want to call, then of course that's fine, but I just want you to know that you're both getting the exact same information at more or less the exact same time, since I plan to express mail both of these as soon as I'm finished writing them.*

*Anyway, the purpose of this letter is that I have a proposal to make. And even though you'll probably not take it very seriously, or think I'm joking (at least when you first start reading), it shouldn't take long for you to realize just how serious I am.*

*And while I realize this may be hard for you to believe, especially in light of my past behavior, not to mention all of the complaining and manipulating I previously engaged in, I am now forced to humbly admit that you guys were completely right in sending me here.*

*Yup, you read that right! I sincerely believe that just by being here and experiencing everything I have, not only have I learned, not only have I grown, but I now truly believe I am not stretching the truth when I say (write) that I'm a much better person than I was when I left.*

*So with that in mind, I would really appreciate it if you would please hear me out, before you go thinking this is just another attempt by me to sway your vote in my favor.*

*So here goes:*

*Right before I left, I heard you guys arguing, and one of you (I don't remember who) mentioned something about Cyber School. And while I'm still not exactly filled in on all of the details, I have to say that over the last few days I've conducted a fair amount of online research, and have found what seems to be a multitude of Virtual Academies to choose from.*

*And even though I've yet to run it by Tally and Tassos (mostly because I wanted to approach you and gain your consent first, which also means that I hope you won't mention it to them before we've had a chance to discuss things), in the end, I think we'll find them to be in full agreement with my plan.*

*So—believe it or not, I've really grown to like it here.*

*I mean, I REALLY like it here.*

*And so I'm wondering if I might be allowed to stay and finish my education by enrolling in Cyber School, since my Greek's not good enough (yet!) to attend the local school.*

*And before you roll your eyes, shake your head, and say NO, please just consider this—if you agree with my plan to let me stay and attend an online school, then:*

1) *Mom—You will be able to move wherever you want. You can even get a one-bedroom apartment, thereby SAVING A TON OF MONEY since you won't have to worry about me, or be forced to stay within my current (high-rent) school district.*

2) *Dad—ALL of these online schools are totally AC-CREDITED and LEGITIMATE, so my dreams of college will not in any way be compromised and/or hindered.*

3) *Also, by staying here, I will become bilingual! A plus on any college and/or job application.*

4) *I will still be able to fly home to visit with both of you on Christmas and New Year's, and you can come visit me for Easter—which happens to be a very big holiday here, and it would be so fun to celebrate it with you! Or even just one of you. Whatever you can arrange.*

5) *And even though online school is not exactly free, I think once you both take the time to sit down and do the math, you will find it to be VERY COST EFFECTIVE.*

6) *Also, just for the record, because I think it needs to be said, Tally and Tassos are NOT CRAZY. They are nice, kind, generous, smart, wonderful people who have become VERY GOOD ROLE MODELS for me (not that you aren't as well).*

7) *Besides, it would only be for the next year. Which, when you think about it, is really just twelve months. Which as you well know, will just fly by before any of us even realizes it's over!*

8) *Not to mention how if I CAN'T return to Harbor High, then I'd really rather just stay here.*

9) *And even if I CAN return to Harbor High, then I'd still rather just stay here.*

10) *And just so you know, this plan practically GUARANTEES both my current and future HAPPINESS. And we all know how important it is to be happy in life.*

*So now that you've taken the time to read my letter, I hope you'll also take the necessary amount of time in which to fully consider my proposal.*

*Though it would also be helpful if you could get back to me as soon as you can, since time is clearly running out.*

*Love,*

*Colby*

*P.S. Dad, I've also decided to send this via e-mail as well as fax it to your office in hopes that you will alert Mom the <u>MO-MENT</u> you receive it, because even though I'm springing for express, one-day airmail, as you can see, time is of the essence.*

August 26
To: NatalieZee
From: ColbyCat
Re: Thanks for the earrings
Hey Nat,

You're not going to believe this, but I'm totally campaigning to get my parents to let me stay in Tinos! I have no idea if they'll actually go for it or not, but I just sent them a very detailed letter making the best case I possibly could, so now I'm just crossing my fingers and hoping for the best.

I mean, it probably sounds weird and all, especially since I started out really hating it here, but even though I'm not sure exactly when or how it happened, I've somehow really grown to like it. And it's NOT just because Yannis and I are back together (though I'm not even sure you knew we were apart, I guess we have a lot to catch up on!), because in just a few weeks he'll be going back to Athens to finish up his last year of high school anyway, which means we'll only be able to see each other on the occasional weekend. But the truth is, I really like this simple, uncluttered, island life. And even though I've made a mess of so many things since I got here (I promise to fill you in on all of that too), somehow my life feels a lot less complicated HERE than it does THERE. No yelling, no fighting, no domestic upheaval, everything's just tranquil, quiet, and peaceful—three things I didn't appreciate until I came here. Not to mention how there's really not much for me to return to, so I guess I just don't see the point in returning at all.

I mean, of course there's still YOU—that is, if we're back to being friends???

But other than that, there's really not much for me to miss, since I'm pretty much over that whole Amanda and Levi scene, so allow me to take a moment to say—You were right! You were right! You were so very right!

Not to mention how I don't even miss any of my "stuff" as much as I originally thought I would—which is pretty weird, since I really, really thought I would.

So anyway, if they let me stay here, then I'll be enrolling in some kind of Cyber School, not sure which one, since there's plenty to choose from. But if not, then it's anyone's guess where I'll end up.

Okay, well, I'm meeting Yannis soon—so, e-mail me back when you can!

Colby

P.S. Oh yeah, I'm so glad you liked the earrings! I made them myself! Though I probably already told you that!

*August 27*

*Dear Tally/Tassos,*

You'll be happy to know that the computer <u>DID NOT CRASH!</u>

*It just ran out of battery, which means you have to plug it in and let it recharge for a while, that's all.*

*If either of my parents (or both!) happen to call—please tell them I'll call them back as soon as I return.*

*But please DO NOT ask them why they are calling, since I already know the reason, and it's kind of private, and not really all that important.*

*Thanks!*

*Love,*

*Colby*

### Colby's Journal for Desperate Times When She's Desperately in Love and Doesn't Care Who Knows

August 29

So yesterday, when I went to the beach with Yannis, I finally worked up the nerve to take off my top! But only because neither Tally nor Tassos nor any of his three hundred cousins were there, which meant we were completely alone (well, other than the other tourists and beachgoers), but even then, I only had it off for like ten seconds, before I put it right back on.

And the second after I did it, Yannis rolled onto his back, squinted at me, and said, "Did you just flash me?"

But I just laughed as my fingers worked at retying my

straps. And once everything was secured, covered, and stowed away safely again, I leaned in and kissed him and said, "Baby steps. You know, one small baby step at a time. That's how you do it. That's how all great change begins."

And as he pulled me down on top of him and started kissing me back, my mind went straight to the pack of condoms I had stashed in my beach bag. And I wondered if we'd end up using them.

Ever since we got back together, it was like I'd become obsessed with the idea of sleeping with Yannis. I mean, not that I hadn't thought about it like a million, gazillion times before, because I had, probably even more than that. But now that we were definitely back together, now that I just might be forced into going home, the whole idea seemed to take on a life of its own, filled with this overwhelming urgency (well, to me anyway, since it's not like he was even aware of it).

Besides, I really, really like him. And even though I used to think I really, really liked Levi, now I realize I was wrong. Because my liking Levi had everything to do with Levi the Image and nothing to do with Levi the Person. I mean, I barely even knew him as a person, and what little I did know, well, I really wasn't all that crazy about. But with Yannis everything is different. We have things in common, we laugh at the same jokes, and we can carry on a conversation just as easily as we can make out.

I guess what I'm trying to say is that Yannis is also like my good friend. And in light of all that, buying a pack of condoms just seemed like the right thing to do.

So the day after Petros's funeral, I got up early, went into town, and purchased a three-pack at the local pharmacy. And I have to admit that the whole entire time my heart was racing, my face was burning, and it was almost as embarrassing as the time I had to buy tampons from this kid in my ninth-grade biology class who was working the register at CVS. But then I reminded myself how I'm not exactly from here, which also meant that the anonymous woman with the furry upper lip who was ringing up my three-pack probably assumed I was just another slutty tourist who she wouldn't think twice about after I left. And even though she did glance from the box to me while raising her eyebrows, I just rolled my eyes and brushed it off, positive I had nothing to worry about.

And the second I walked out of that store, with the small brown bag clutched tightly in my fist, the contraband condoms secured in my possession, the specifics of just <u>HOW</u> and <u>WHEN</u> I would actually go about using them became pretty much all I could think about.

Seriously, it's like every morning I wake up, I can't help but think:

*Will today be the day I sleep with Yannis?*

And since time is seriously running out, I was starting to think that today was probably as good a day as any.

Though it's not like I'd planned to do it right there on the beach.

Yet, wouldn't you know it, just as I was really getting

into kissing him back, I accidentally kicked my bag with my foot, which made the whole thing tip over, which made all the contents spill across the sand. And it's not like I even would've stopped kissing him long enough to notice, except that when Yannis came up for air, he also started to clean up the mess.

And when he came to the small, silver packet, he looked at me, and said, "So you really did buy condoms. I thought they were making a joke."

"What?" I gasped, sitting up so fast an entire constellation of stars swirled before my eyes, watching, in complete mortification, as the little packet, my most embarrassing purchase ever, dangled from the tips of his fingers.

"Christos told me," he said, the condoms swinging back and forth in a rush of silver, as though I was being hypnotized. "But I think it was Georgos who told him. But actually, it all started with Katerina, Maria's aunt. She's the one who owns the pharmacy."

"Your LITTLE BROTHER told you I bought condoms?" I asked, going straight to the most horrifying on the LIST OF PEOPLE WHO KNOW I BOUGHT CONDOMS, as I frantically tried to wrap my mind around how this could possibly ever have happened. I mean, wasn't there some kind of law against this? Wasn't there some kind of INTERNATIONAL PROPHYLAC-TIC PURCHASING PRIVACY ACT? And if not, WHY not? "And who's Georgos? Do you mean YOUR COUSIN Georgos? And is that the Maria I'm thinking of?" My eyes were bulging, my palms sweating, my heart racing, my mind spinning, watching as Yannis just nodded, clearly amused.

"You mean the WHOLE TOWN, no, scratch that, you mean the WHOLE ISLAND, knows I bought condoms?" I yelped, clearly on the verge of hysteria.

He nodded again. "And now the entire beach too," he added, laughing and glancing around at all the surrounding gawkers.

"Oh my God, this is NOT HAPPENING! It's too horrible!" I buried my face in my hands, unable to look at him, unable to look at anyone, possibly ever again.

But he just laughed. "That's Tinos," he said. "You sure you still want to live here?"

"What's that supposed to mean?" I asked, lifting my head and peering at him, my eyes searching his face, wondering where this was leading. Did he not want me to stay? Had he changed his mind—about me, about us? And if so, was it because I'm the kind of girl who buys condoms?

"Colby," he said, dropping the stupid, silver package and cupping my face in his hands. "Things are different here. It's not like what you're used to back home. The island is small, everyone knows each other, and people like to talk."

"I'll say." I rolled my eyes, wondering how I'd ever face those nasty gossips again, not to mention his brother and cousin, and so on.

"Think of it like high school. Or at least the way you described American high school to me. Only here, high school is not so—contained to one place. High school is where you live, all of the time, and there's no escaping it. Ask your aunt Tally, she'll tell you."

"Tally knows I bought condoms too?" I said, thinking how it just seemed to get worse and worse, wondering if the list would ever end.

But he just laughed. "Probably. But what I meant to say was, she knows just how small this place can be. Why don't you ask her about it sometime? You two never really talk, do you?"

And the moment he said it, I felt kind of angry. I mean, who was he to act like he knew something about Tally that I didn't? I'm the one who just spent nearly three months living with her. But just as I was about to defend myself, and let him know how we happen to talk all the time, I realized he was right. We didn't talk much at all. And when I really stopped and thought about it, I actually knew very little about her. Of course, I knew her likes and dislikes, was fully indoctrinated in all of her wacky beliefs, but I guess I didn't really know all that much about her personal history. I didn't really know much about HER. So in the end, I just looked at him and shrugged. But little did I know it was about to get worse.

Because then he looked at me and said, "And Colby, I want you to know that you don't have to do this."

"Do what?" I asked, my head spinning with so many things, I was no longer sure what he might mean.

Then he gazed down at the condoms and back at me, and it didn't take a mind reader to know what he was getting at.

"You mean—you don't want to?" I asked, unable to hide my shock. I mean, the whole entire time I'd been obsessing over it, I was sure the final decision would be mine and mine alone. I never even considered he might have a say.

But he just shrugged. And the moment I saw it, the second I witnessed that casual rise and fall of his shoulders, my face burned with shame, my heart filled with humiliation, and I reached for that stupid package with fingers so shaky and hectic I was sure I would drop it. But then I picked it right up and tossed it back in my bag, making a big show of hurling my sunscreen, books, and magazines right on top, ensuring it stayed out of sight, buried, forgotten underneath.

Then just as I reached for my T-shirt, thinking it was as good a time as any to leave, he placed his hand on my arm and said, "*Koukla Mou,* please don't go."

And I caved. Completely folded, cried uncle, and tossed my T-shirt aside. Basically because ever since we got back together, I cannot resist when he calls me that. But that doesn't mean I wasn't annoyed.

Then he looked at me and said, "What I meant was, you don't have to do this for me. Or because you think I want to do it. Or because you think you might be leaving soon, and that you'll never see me again, and so you have to do it. Or because you think that if you don't do it, then I might forget you. Because even though I want to do it, Colby, more than you will ever know, none of these reasons are very good for you. And I don't want you to do something that you might someday regret."

"Why would I regret it?" I said, feeling totally, inexplicably annoyed. I mean, it wasn't natural, wasn't normal. What guy turns down the opportunity to have sex? Who in their right mind does that?

But he just laughed. "Well, you can be a little impulsive, in case you haven't noticed."

I rolled my eyes. Because even though that may well be the case, what was it to him? I mean, what did he care if I lived to regret it? Chances were we'd never see each other again anyway, so what then? I mean, I definitely regretted the first time, but somehow I managed to get through that. So what's the big deal if the second time turns out to be an even bigger mistake? But no sooner had I thought it, than I realized that was pretty much what he was getting at to begin with. That it was completely and entirely possible to avoid future regret, if you stopped long enough to really think things through.

So then I looked at him and said, "Well, maybe you're right. But then again, since the whole town thinks we're already doing it, don't you think we should maybe just go ahead and do it?" And then I laughed, but not a real laugh, just my stupid nervous laugh, the one he was probably very familiar with by now.

But he just smiled, and leaned in to kiss me. "We have three more nights together," he whispered, his lips moving against mine. "Take some time to think about it, and then let me know. Really, it's no worries."

I looked at him for a moment, then I shook my head, pulled away, and lay back on my towel. "You're a really weird guy, you know that?" I said, turning my head to peer at him.

But he just smiled. "So you tell me."

August 29
To: CarlCavendish
From: ColbyCat
Re: Is that your final answer?
Dad:

I just got home and read Tally's note saying you will see me at the airport on the thirty-first of August and I'm taking that to mean either:

1) You haven't received my prior e-mail, fax, and/or letter and therefore are unaware of the other, very reasonable and valid options I have presented. **<u>OR:</u>**

2) You are familiar with all of the other options, but for some reason that is not only unclear to me but that I cannot possibly begin to fathom, have chosen to reject them.

Please advise me of your position at your earliest convenience.

And in the event that you have chosen to reject my proposal, then I need to know if this was a decision made jointly (between you and Mom) or if it's one you have taken the liberty to decide on your own, unbeknownst to Mom.

Love,

Your daughter who is in desperate need of clarification,

Colby

P.S. I am attaching a list of relevant Web sites for your perusal. Please take the time to view them.


August 29

To: CarlCavendish

From: ColbyCat

Re: Is that your final answer?

Dad,

I assure you that I am not "horsing around." I am completely serious, and was hoping you would take me seriously too. Cyber School, Online Education, Virtual Academy, call it what you will, it is definitely NOT a joke. It is a valid, legitimate education option, as all of the schools are ACCREDITED. Which, I might add, if you'd actually taken the time to look over those Web sites I forwarded to you, then you would know that by now.

And furthermore, I don't see how you can possibly be in a position to make any kind of decision for my future when you are so clearly closed off to all of the options but one. And while I'm sorry to say it, I think you should know that I'm very disappointed, not to mention shocked by the unjust unfairness of it all. I am also both saddened and upset to see the way you are handling my life in such a cavalier and random manner.

So I ask you again, would you PLEASE just do me the favor of taking TEN MINUTES out of your very busy day, and click on the links that I sent you in the last e-mail and that I am attaching again in this e-mail. And then pick up the phone and CALL MOM, so that the two of you, TOGETHER, can take a calm, rational, logical, inclusive approach to the one and only thing I need to secure a happy and successful future.

That's ALL I ask.

Love,

Colby

August 29
To: CarlCavendish
From: ColbyCat
Re: Is that your final answer?
Dad,

Fine.

See you on the thirty-first.

Colby

August 30
To: AmandaStar
From: ColbyCat
Re: Yo, Bitch!
Hey Amanda,

I know. You are so totally right. NOBODY gets away with talking/writing to you the way I did.

Though maybe you should let them, because you just might learn something.

But no worries, since it's not like we'll be talking all that much in the future anyway. Partly because I'm back to being best friends with Nat, but mostly because there's just not much point in us talking to each other anyway.

So—all the best to you—see you around Harbor. (That's right, I'll be back!)

Colby

August 30
To: NatalieZee
From: ColbyCat
Re: Home sweet home
Hey Nat,

I'll keep this short and sweet since I've only got one day left here in Tinos and I don't want to waste it on the computer since I've wasted way too many days like that already. So here's the short list of things you need to know:

1) Cyber School is out. Apparently my parents are even more close-minded than I ever could've imagined. Oh well, at least I tried.

2) Harbor is in! That's right, read it and weep! My mom found an apartment for us, and we're moving in next month!

3) I may or may not sleep with Yannis. Which means tonight could turn out to be a VERY BIG NIGHT—or not. It re-

mains to be seen. . . . Either way, I'll give you all the details when I see you! There's so much to tell!

4) I just want to take the time to say that I'm really glad we're still friends, and that next year is totally gonna rock! Even if Amanda does totally hate me and will probably do her best to sabotage me and/or take me down every chance she gets. (Like #3, I'll explain when I see you.).

See you soon!
Colby

### Colby's Journal for Desperate Times When She'll Soon Have to Start a New Journal

August 31

It's funny to think how at the beginning of this summer, back when I was still in California, and my mom gave me this journal, I was sure I wouldn't even crack it open, much less start writing in it. But now that the summer's almost over, and I'm about to head home, I've managed to fill up nearly every page.

I guess I was just so mad about being sent here I'd convinced myself that I couldn't possibly experience anything worth writing about.

And now I'm just glad I was wrong.

So today (well I guess it's technically yesterday, but whatever), anyway, so in light of it being my last day and all, Tally and Tassos planned to throw a big going-away BBQ for me. But I guess I should backtrack and say that first, way before the party, we decided to spend the day at the beach. But just Tally and me since Tassos was busy working on a big sculpture that some guy in France commissioned, and Yannis had to work at the hotel. And even though I felt kind of bad that I'd been too wrapped up in myself to do it before, I figured it was better late than never, so I dove right in and asked Tally about her life.

And as it turns out, I learned a lot. Stuff I never knew, stuff I never could've imagined.

Like:

1) She met Tassos the very first day she arrived in Tinos. And just like Yannis and me the first time they saw each other was on the boat. But unlike Yannis and me they actually spoke on the boat. Because when Tally accidentally knocked over her coffee, Tassos was sitting beside her and offered to help clean it up. But even though she said she thought he was cute, it wasn't until two years later that they actually got together. Partly because she said she was reluctant to date anyone so soon after her divorce, and partly because Tassos was totally grieving over his daughter's suicide.

2) That's right, Tassos was also married before, and he had a seventeen-year-old daughter who died of an overdose. Only it wasn't an

accident, and they happen to know this because she left a note. Though I have no idea
what the note said, and believe me, it's not
like I asked. Anyway, I have to admit that
hearing that really freaked me out. I mean,
his daughter was the same age when she died
as I am right now, and even though at one
point I thought my life was just about as bad
as it gets, I guess it was never really all that
bad after all.

3) So apparently, not long after the overdose, Tassos and his wife split. Tally said they were both
really sad, and angry, and sort of lashed out and
blamed each other. And right after they got divorced, his wife moved back to Sweden (where
she's from) and Tassos quit his job in Athens
(apparently he was an airline executive—which
trust me, I NEVER would've imagined, because he is so NOT the buttoned-up, super serious, suit-wearing, type A, type!) and moved
back to Tinos, where he's originally from, and
enrolled in the famous marble sculpting school
they have here, determined to follow his pas-
sion, try to be happy again, and live a life that
mattered, or something like that.

4) But when he came back to Tinos, he was surprised at how everyone was gossiping about
him and saying some not-so-nice things
about him, his wife, and his daughter, until

he eventually became so depressed and dis-
traught, he became like a total recluse, barely
leaving his house.

5)  Then one day Tally and Tassos ran into each other
at the agricultural co-op and it wasn't long after
that when they started living together, which
made people talk even more, because shacking
up is pretty much frowned upon here. But they
both agreed to live their lives like they want and
not to care about what anyone else thinks.

And then, I guess because we were kind of on a sharing binge, she told me how she knew all about the condoms I'd bought.

And I felt myself turn every shade of red, even though
I'm actually really, really tan, which means she probably
couldn't even tell that I was blushing. But still, I felt so
embarrassed I could hardly even look at her (and believe
me, this time it had nothing to do with the fact that she
was, once again, topless).

And then she asked me if we needed to, as she put it,
"Have a little talk."

So I said, "Well, apparently not, since *I'm* the one who
was smart enough to buy the condoms."

And then we both laughed.

And when she asked me whether or not I was planning
to use the condoms, I looked her right in the eye and told
her the truth. "I have no idea," I said. "I guess we'll just see
how it goes."

And even though I hadn't planned on sharing anything more than that, even though I really thought I'd gotten over it already, before I even realized what I was doing, I started telling her all about that night with Levi, and how ashamed and stupid I felt after, and how lately I was thinking that maybe sleeping with Yannis could somehow erase it, or at the very least, correct it.

And then I just kept going, telling her all about how I dumped Natalie so I could hang with Amanda, about everything that happened (and didn't happen) in Mykonos, and how lately I'd been feeling so confused, like I had one foot in Tinos and the other in California, and I just wasn't sure where I fit anymore. How when I was in Mykonos, all I did was judge Levi and his family for their predictable American ways, and how the night before that I'd judged Yannis for being so quintessentially Greek. But how really, deep down inside, I knew the real problem was me.

But she just looked at me and smiled when she said, "Colby, there's no right way or wrong way, there's just your way. And you'll be a whole lot happier when you figure out what that is."

"But that's the thing," I said, feeling immediately frustrated by her usual obscure statements.

But she just shrugged and said, "You can never go wrong when you act from love."

Well, shortly after that I got up from my towel and waded deep into the sea, going so far out I was forced to stand on the very tips of my toes in order to breathe. Then I tilted my head back, closed my eyes, and let the water support me, thinking how there were few greater feelings than that—of being so light and free you were hardly even aware of yourself.

I stayed like that for a long time, partly because it felt far too good to stop, but mostly because I was reluctant to head back to shore, back to the gravity of my body, my life, my choices.

But as I allowed myself to float some more I thought: *Maybe I'm still overthinking everything. Maybe I'm still trying to control stuff that's out of my control. Maybe I should act the same way on land as I do in the sea, learn to let go, to aim for what I want without trying to force it so much. Just see where the current leads me, since it's not like I'm not a good swimmer, it's not like I can't find my way back to shore.*

And when I climbed out of the water and headed for my towel, I told Tally I was ready to head back home and prepare for my going away.

By the time we got back, Tassos was already there, marinating the meats, chopping vegetables, peeling potatoes, and basically handling all of the party prep duties. So after taking a quick shower and changing into a new dress I bought in town a few days before (a day which will forever be known as <u>CONDOM DAY</u>), I headed outside to help.

And while I was setting the tables and rearranging the chairs, I happened to mention how sorry I was about his daughter.

At first, with the way he looked at me, his eyes so startled and wide, I immediately regretted bringing it up. But then he nodded slowly and said, "Tally told you?"

I nodded. "But please don't be mad, because—"

But he just shook his head. "I'm not mad, Colby."

And as I started lighting the candles, he put on a Jackson Browne CD, and then I turned to him again and said, "Do you blame yourself?"

And even though he just shrugged, it was obvious he did.

I held the match, watching as the flame crept near my fingers, inching dangerously close before I shook it out and said, "Well, you shouldn't."

He looked at me and smiled. "I know."

And even though I should've just let it end there, I had something more to say, so I looked at him and added, "I just want you to know that you and Tally have really helped me this summer."

Then his eyes grew wet and mine started to sting, so I started slicing potatoes as he turned to prepare the salad.

It wasn't long after that when all the guests started arriving, and even though it still surprises me to write this (never mind having lived it), I'm proud to say that this time I made sure both Maria and Christina were invited. I guess I just didn't see the point in trying to keep them away. And even though we didn't exactly hang out together, and even though they were probably pretty happy that it was my GOING-AWAY party, it just didn't matter anymore.

So after way too much food, a good amount of dancing, a little bit of drinking, and an endless amount of laughing, I hugged every single person good-bye (yes, including Maria and Christina), and after they'd gone, Tally and Tassos hugged me and Yannis good night, then Tally looked at me and said, "Stay up as long as you want. But just remember you have a ferry to catch in the morning."

Then they both went to bed, and Yannis and I remained on the terrace, both of us acting so weird and nervous that any casual observer would swear we'd just met.

"Well, that was a fun party," he said, smiling at me in this polite, formal way.

"Yes it was," I answered, feeling inexplicably awkward, then adding, "a really fun party." Which made me roll my eyes, shake my head, and cringe.

"Should we go for a ride?" he finally asked, his voice sounding thick and uncertain, suspended in silence.

I nodded, my stomach feeling all jumpy and weird as he reached for my hand, my eyes searching his face when I asked, "To our beach?"

But he just smiled and helped me climb onto the back of his Vespa.

This time when we ended up at the hotel, I can't say I was all that surprised, but when he led me up to the pool, I was surprised to see it filled.

"Want to go for a swim?" he asked, busying himself with lighting the large, oversize lanterns that were scattered all around.

"I forgot my suit," I said, kneeling down near the edge, dipping my fingers into the water, surprised to find it cool, but inviting.

"That didn't stop you before." He smiled, blowing out the match now that the candles were all lit.

And even though I still hadn't made up my mind about exactly how the night would end, I also knew I should stop thinking about it, and just see where it led.

So I pulled off my dress and dove right in. And not five seconds later, Yannis had joined me.

We swam, and played, and kissed, and swam some more, and by the time we'd climbed out and were wrapped in large towels, he took one look at me and said, "You look just like you did the day I first saw you, only happier."

And when I rubbed my towel over my face and saw how it came away all streaked with mascara, I couldn't help but laugh.

Then he grabbed my hand and led me through the lobby, and up a narrow stairway to a large second-floor suite. And when he opened the door and motioned me inside, I saw there were more candles, a CD player, and a fully made bed.

"I didn't realize you'd finished all the rooms," I said, going over to part the dark blue drapes, gazing out at what should've been the view if the night hadn't been so dark.

"They're not finished," he said, coming up behind me and nuzzling the back of my neck. "Only this one."

"But what about your parents? Won't they get mad?" I asked, knowing how traditional the Greeks could be, trying not to think about getting caught.

Alyson Noël

But he just shrugged. "It's different for boys. If I was a girl, then yes, it would be a problem."

"Is that why I haven't met your parents?" I asked, thinking it was a weird time to be having this conversation, but still, I was nervous, unsure, and it was something I'd been wondering anyway. "Because they wouldn't approve of me?" I continued, wondering if he'd answer honestly, or just try to hedge and stall and beat around the bush.

But he just laughed. "You have met my parents. Well, you've met my father, you just didn't know it."

I turned to look at him, my mind racing, trying to recall when that could've been.

"The day you came to the hotel to yell at me." He smiled.

"Which one was your father?" I asked, remembering the group of workers, how they'd laughed and elbowed each other when I'd asked where he was, all of them too young to be his dad. Well, all except for one.

"He brought you to me."

"Oh, great." I closed my eyes and turned away. "That's just great. No wonder you never bothered to introduce me to your mother." I shook my head, wondering if his dad had eavesdropped by the door, listening to every stupid thing I'd said. "So, go ahead, lay it on me, what did he say? What was the verdict? Does he think I'm a freak?" I held my breath and waited.

"Does it matter?" Yannis asked, whispering the words in my ear.

I just shrugged, even though I was beginning to think that it did.

He sighed. "Well, if you really must know, he told me that I should be careful with you. That I should have fun, but be careful."

"Careful of what?" I asked, turning to look at him again.

"He said you might try to get pregnant and wreck my life."

I rolled my eyes. "Please, did you tell him that *I'm* the one who bought the condoms? Oh wait, never mind, I'm sure he already knows, heck, all of Tinos knows."

Yannis shrugged. "I told you things are different here, relationships aren't so—casual as where you live. Here, when two people date, everyone starts talking about marriage. It's better not to bring anyone home until things are serious."

I looked away, torn between worrying that we were just a casual summer fling, one that he'd soon forget, and wondering if I really wanted it to be anything more.

Then I looked at him and asked, "Are we casual?"

But he just smiled and pulled me toward the bed, his lips moving softly against my ear as he whispered, "Come with me, *koukla mou*."

*August 31*
*Dear Mom and Dad,*
*You may notice that this letter is written on a coffee-stained Ellas Ferry Lines napkin (not unlike a previous note I sent several*

*months ago). Well, that's because I'm on the ferry to Mykonos. So that I can then fly to Athens, so that I can then fly to Frankfurt, so that I can then fly to New York, so that I can then land in L.A., so that you can then pick me up and drive me home.*

*But unlike my last napkin letter, this one is not angry.*

*In fact, it's not even close.*

*Because believe it or not, I'm actually looking forward to seeing you (an event that will happen long before you receive this, but I'm mailing it anyway), so that I can thank you for packing me up and shipping me off to spend the summer with my CRAZY AUNT TALLY in Tinos.*

*It was an amazing experience.*

*Love,*

*Colby*

*P.S. Mom, just so you know, the ONLY reason I'm sending this to Dad's address and not to yours is because I know we'll be moving soon and I'm not sure if you've started forwarding the mail yet, and since I don't want this to get lost . . . Anyway, that is the one and only reason, and I just wanted you to know that so you won't think I'm playing favorites. Hope this part of the note doesn't upset you, I just wanted to make myself clear.* ☺

### Colby's Journal for Desperate Times When She's Stuck at 37,000 Feet and There Is No Internet Access and She's Almost Out of Paper

August 31

I tried, I really, really tried. But somehow I still ended up on this airplane, in seats 24G and H (got two to myself! Yipee!), far enough away from the bathroom that I don't have to suffer that pervasive God-awful smell, but still next to the window so that I can lift my shade and look out at—

### <u>EVERYTHING!</u>

Because even though each passing second takes me farther and farther from where I'd really rather be, there's just something so cool about looking out at the sun and the moon and the endless blue sky and thinking—

That's the same sky Yannis sees!

That's the same sun that warms both our skin!

And every night when we go outside, we can both

look up and gaze at the exact same moon! (Granted, ten

hours apart.)

All of which means we're not as far apart as it seems. That no matter where I end up, no matter where I go from here, in some vast, eternal way, we'll always be connected.

And even though I'd give just about anything to be with him now, I'm also determined to be perfectly okay with my choices—even the ones that are made for me.

Like last night, when Yannis and I slept together. In the end, we didn't <u>ACTUALLY</u> sleep together.

And it's not like I didn't want to, and it's not like I wasn't ready, because I was. In fact, I really, <u>REALLY</u> wanted to, and I really did feel ready. And without being too graphic, I think I can say that he was ready too.

And even though I'd made up my mind to go through with it, even though I'd convinced myself that the time was perfectly right, at this one point, when we were lying on our sides, facing each other, he brought his hand to my cheek, tucked my hair behind my ear, looked straight into my eyes and said, "*S'agapo,* Colby."

And unlike the last time when I wasn't at all ready to hear it, much less feel it or share it, I gazed right back at him, and said, "I love you too, Yannis."

And somehow, just allowing myself to not only hear the words, but also to accept them, and say them right back, felt so huge, so monumental, and so overwhelmingly good—that I just wanted to hold on to it. I wanted to keep it, and savor it, and enjoy it for what it was.

And I didn't want it to compete with anything else.

And even though it probably sounded pretty weird and stupid when I tried to explain that to him, he just pulled me into his arms, pressed his lips to my forehead, and assured me it was plenty enough for him too.

Then we slept, all wrapped up in each other's arms, and I felt so good, and so safe, and so complete, that I didn't wake up until it was way, way late.

"Oh my God! Oh crap!" I yelled, jumping out of bed and frantically pulling on my dress. Not realizing I was wearing it backward 'til I started shoving my feet in my shoes.

"Yannis! Get up!" I cried, shaking his shoulder, before searching the room for my purse. "You have to take me to the port! No! Wait! You have to take me home so Tally and Tassos can take me to the port! Only, you're coming too, right?" I stopped long enough to look at him, hoping that my mascara-streaked face, backward dress, and fright-wig hair would not be his very last impression of me.

But Yannis was already dressed, his keys in one hand, funky, weird sandals in the other, as he opened the door, smiled, and said, "Relax, it's no worries."

And I broke out laughing. Bent over, side-clutching laughing. I mean, I could hardly believe how dumb I'd been to almost miss out on LOVE all because of some awkward-sounding slang and an odd pair of sandals. And even though I tried to stop, I just couldn't. So he grabbed me by the arm and pulled me out the door and over to his bike, muttering, "Crazy California girl," as he got me safely settled onto the back.

And by the time we got to Tally's, I completely panicked again when I saw that Tally and Tassos were not even there! But as it turns out, they were out looking for me. Starting at our secret make-out beach (which apparently was not such a secret, but hey, that's small town island living for ya) and ending at the port, where they confirmed my boat was ready and waiting, although I was not yet on it. And by the time they got back to the house, I was sitting in the drive, bags packed and ready, allowing them five more minutes to show before I'd leave without them.

So I climbed in the back of the jeep, as Yannis followed behind on his bike, and we all caravanned down to the port. And even though I fully admit that the whole entire time I was hoping for some sort of nautical malfunction, or horrendous, catastrophic summer storm—something to keep my boat from sailing so I'd have no choice but to stay put—in the end, I was greeted with a perfectly clear, Meltemi-free day. Which I pretty much took as a sign that, like it or not, I was destined to leave.

And by the time we parked and made our way down to the dock my boat was already well into loading mode, which didn't really leave much time for good-bye. But then again, that's probably also a good thing since I've never been much good at final moments anyway.

So after hugging Tassos, and basically thanking him for <u>EVERYTHING,</u> I leaned in to hug Tally, and burst out crying so fast and hard, I could hardly even believe it. But she just let me cling to her, as she ran her hand over my hair, whispering, "It's okay, it's all going to be okay."

And when I finally pulled away, I wiped my eyes, and smiled, and said, "I know."

And then we promised to stay in touch and e-mail each other as often as we could, and then I made some dumb joke about how if they needed any help in figuring out the e-mail then they could just e-mail me and let me know. And even though it was totally lame, and obviously not at all funny, it really helped ease all of the tension and sadness, so we all laughed anyway.

After hugging them again, I walked the rest of the way with Yannis, holding hands as we made our way toward the gangway, but then Yannis suddenly stopped and said, "Colby, isn't that—?"

I gazed in the direction he was pointing, not sure if he was right until I saw the beaded collar, then I knew for sure. He'd grown, since I'd last seen him, <u>A LOT.</u> But still, between the collar, the shiny black coat, and the cute little white streak, I knew I was looking at Holly.

"Where are you going?" I asked, watching as Yannis charged toward the little dark-haired girl in the bright yellow sundress, the one who was cradling Holly, singing in his ear as she stroked his shiny dark fur.

"What do you mean? That's YOUR cat, Colby, I'm going to get him back!" he said, walking that much faster.

I grabbed his arm, making him stop long enough to face me. "No, Yannis, please. Just leave him," I said, not knowing if I really meant it until the moment it was out.

But Yannis just shook his head and started off again, saying, "No worries, she's the daughter of my cousin, I can get her another one."

But again, I grabbed his arm, forcing him to look at me as I said, "No, Yannis, I'm serious."

His eyes searched my face, his expression showing just how crazy he thought I was. "But why? I don't understand. I thought you said you missed him? I thought you wanted him back?"

"I did miss him, and I did want him back." I nodded. "Until now."

Yannis narrowed his eyes, gazing at me.

"Just look," I said. "*Really* look."

So he did. And then he turned to me and shrugged. "I don't get it. It is Holly, right?"

"Yes, and look at the way that little girl is holding him, how he's pressed up so tight against her chest, and how her arms are wrapped so snugly around him. Look at how he lets her do that. He never did that with me. Not once. With me he always scratched and struggled to be free."

"He's older now," Yannis said, shaking his head and squinting.

But I just shook my head and smiled. "No Yannis, he's home."

By the time we got to the gangway, we kissed so long the boat nearly sailed without me. But in the end, I'm glad we managed to keep it honest and real, that we managed to say good-bye, and say "I love you," without forcing a bunch of false promises on each other, ones we might not be able to keep.

Because the only thing that was certain was that we loved each other, that we had each other's e-mail address, and that we'd see where it led.

Because if there's one thing I now know for sure, it's that nothing is ever sure.

## CIRCLE IN THE SAND

September 7

Well, I guess this blog title was more appropriate than I realized way back when I chose it, since I really have come full circle, and now I'm right back where I started. Even though almost everything is different from the way I left it. But since circles have no end, I guess it's really just the beginning of another cycle, and who knows where that'll lead?

But in order to keep you up to date, let me just say that by the time I made it to LAX I was completely, and totally, exhausted. But even though I was so tired I could barely keep my eyes open it was still pretty great to see both my parents, standing side by side, no legal counsel in sight, and with no obvious grievances (at least none that I could see), both of them looking relaxed and happy to see me—just as I was happy to see them.

And since I knew better than to hug one of them before the other, I just walked right up, with my arms spread wide, pretty much forcing them into a big group hug. And even though they resisted at first, after a moment or two, they finally let go, and gave in. And the second I pulled away, I couldn't help but think of Tally, since she's the one who taught me how to deal with resistance.

And even after explaining how I'd spent the last twenty-some hours snacking on candy bars, potato chips, and just about anything else that could be shrink-wrapped and sold in an airport gift shop, they still insisted on taking me to dinner. Which meant it was time for me to stop resisting and give in to them.

And although there's like a ton of things to write, I'm just too busy with unpacking all of my boxes and decorating my new room—not to mention how school's starting up in less than a week—so in light of all that, I thought I'd leave you with these photos, provide a little commentary, and let you draw your own conclusions.

1) That's a picture of my old room. Though of course it wasn't empty like that when I occupied it! I guess I just didn't really think to take a picture until I'd already packed everything up for the big move. But it's weird how seeing it looking so bare and abandoned like that makes me realize how in the end, it was never anything more than just four walls, a door, a closet, and a window. Which makes me feel kind of dumb for allowing myself to get so attached to it. And if you need any further explanation on just what exactly I mean, then please feel free to check out photo #2.

2) So what we have here, ladies and gentlemen, is basically four walls, a door, a closet, and a window. Which also happens to be all of the elements that make up my new room. Which means it's not all that different from my old room. And even though the carpet's a little plain for my taste, my aunt Tally promised to send me one of those cool, Greek flokati rugs like I had in my room at her place, you know, just to jazz it up a little (and remind me of my other home!). Which just goes to show that HOME, like PARADISE, is really just a state of mind.

3) That's my best friend, Nat, who was kind and generous enough to dedicate her one and only day off (well, this week anyway) from her job at the *You've Been Framed!* art supply shop to help me unpack most, though not all, of my boxes (but only because there turned out to be far more than either of us bargained for, which, I have to admit, has made me reconsider my aunt Tally's philosophy toward accumulation and mass consumerism, as I can't help but wonder if she just might be on to something!). Nat also helped me organize my closet and drawers, which is so incredibly nice of her and lucky for me since she's really good at "spatial relations" (her words, not mine). Notice the uber-cool earrings she's wearing? I made those ones too!

4) That's a picture of my dad, his girlfriend, Melanie, and me having dinner at the condo he just bought. And even though it wasn't really necessary, since it's not that far from the apartment, I still ended up staying the night because they were sweet enough to go to the trouble to decorate my room, and they were anxious for me to try it out.

5) This is a picture of my room at my dad's place. Notice the boy band picture on the wall? Well, just so you know, it's no longer there. Because Melanie and I took it down, then snuck it into my dad's office and hung it up behind his desk when he was in a

meeting, since both of us are convinced that he's the one who secretly likes boy band music!

6) This is a picture of Mr. Holly Golightly that Yannis sent me all the way from Tinos. Just so you know, Holly is now living with his cousin's little eight-year-old daughter, Tatiana, and he seems to be quite happy and very well fed from what I can see. And Yannis continues to visit every now and then just so he can whisper in Holly's ear and make sure he never forgets me.

7) This is a picture of Harbor High School, that was taken the day Nat and I stopped by because she was so excited about the new art lab she just couldn't wait until school started. I don't know if I mentioned this before, but Nat is REALLY into art. She likes to paint, no, actually, she LIVES to paint, and she's really good at it too. She's also good friends with the art teacher (yup, she's the kind of girl who makes friends with her teachers, what can I say?), and by the time we left I'd decided to switch one of my electives to an art class too. They have this pottery class I didn't even know about, but now that I do, I'm really hoping they'll let me switch.

8) This is a picture of Amanda, Jenna, Levi, and Casey, who we just happened to run into that very same day, since the guys were there for football practice and the girls were there to watch them. And even though I'm not positive, I kind of think

Amanda and Levi might be together now, since she seemed a little disturbed when he came over to talk to me. But I am totally sure that Jenna and Casey are together, mostly because they were hanging all over each other. Though you know how these things go, and by the time you read this they could have totally switched back, or moved on to someone else entirely. And while I have to admit that it felt really awkward to run into them at first, in the end, we pretty much just said hey, shared some news, and went our separate ways.

And that's it!

So if anyone is actually out there and reading this—then don't forget to comment!

Love,

Colby

## CIRCLE IN THE SAND

**Blog Comments:**

**Tinian Arts said:**

We mailed the rug today, so expect to receive it in a few weeks!

We both really miss you—the house is so quiet without you!

Love,

Tally & Tassos

**Natalie Zee said:**

Yup, I'm a big art-fart dork who makes friends with her teachers, and now the whole world knows! Are we still on for tonight? My art show starts at eight—I'm so nervous!

**ColbyCat said:**

I'm just about to upload one of your paintings so "the whole world" can see how awesome they are! See you at eight! Don't sweat it—you'll be great!

**Anonymous said:**

I'm still here, still reading your blog, still missing you.

**ColbyCat said:**

And still ANONYMOUS?

**Anonymous said:**

Hopefully not to you.

**ColbyCat said:**

DEFINITELY not to me.

**Anonymous said:**

By the way, our moon is half full tonight.

**ColbyCat said:**

I'm heading out now.

**Anonymous said:**

Kalinichta!

**ColbyCat said:**

Kalinichta!